AXEL

The Mysterious Tapestry

ADELPHA L. DeGUZMAN

This is a work of fiction. Any references to historical events, real people or real places are used fictionally. Any similarity to names, characters, places and events are products of the author's imagination. Any semblance to actual events, places or persons are purely coincidental.

Copyright© 2023 by Adelpha L.DeGuzman.

All rights reserved. No part of this book may be reproduced in any form or by any electronic or mechanical means including information storage and retrieval system without written permission from the author or publisher.

Acknowledgement

As an immigrant, writing a book seemed so impossible for me to accomplish in the United States but fulfilling this lifelong dream was made possible only with the full support of my husband Athene D. DeGuzman, my daughter Bernadette L. DeGuzman and my sister Aloha L. Francisco. They helped me every step of the way, erased my self-doubts and encouraged me to finish every chapter and finally this project.

I dedicate this book to my granddaughter, Alex D. Stouffer for being my inspiration to start this novel.

I want to give special thanks to my daughter Christine L. DeGuzman for her insights into how young adults generally think and express themselves. She helped me bridge the big generational linguistic gap from my age to create a novel that would be enjoyed by young and old alike.

As a novice in writing, I want to give thanks to Kim Beales (YourBookMarketers.com) who supported me through this process and all my friends who encouraged me to fulfill my dream.

— CHAPTER 1 —

The Fair

The normally quiet Central Plaza in the northeastern New England town of Moons Borough was abuzz with activity. People from near and far came swarming like ants to the village circle for the biggest event of the year: the annual New Year's Eve party a year after the turn of the millennium.

In the beginning, this small community was created as a farming settlement. Most residents tended vegetables and fruit trees around their homes. Richer folks focused on raising pigs, chickens, and cows. They rode horses to check on their properties and transport their products. Even children helped by watering the plants, feeding the animals, and milking the cows.

As the town grew, the farmers set up stalls to sell their produce and livestock. Over time, as carriages went away and roads were paved for cars, more people settled in the area. George Moon, who founded the town, was its first official mayor. He designed the plaza to be the main marketplace. A road was carved around the center, creating a roundabout with six smaller streets radiating out to connect to the rest of the town. From an aerial view, the sight of the lit plaza resembled the rays of the sun chasing away the dark embrace of the night.

To the west outside the plaza, there were parking spaces for visitors, while in the south and east, residential homes sparsely dotted the landscape toward the mountain. The church, hospital, and several business offices mostly occupied the northern section of the town.

A pathway paved with gray cobblestones led visitors toward the entrance of the plaza. Blue and purple irises, traditionally believed to be local symbols of hope and wisdom, adorned the hedge fence, and a brilliant white entryway welcomed everyone.

At the foot of the entrance, the Knight family could barely contain their excitement to join the festivities inside. As soon as the dad opened the gate, two girls dashed into the cacophony of sights, smells, and sounds. Straw crunched under the girls' feet, as they darted off. Their father, Charles, was overwhelmed by the sweet smell of funnel cakes and apple pies. Their mother, Sarah, yelled at them to slow down and followed along, carefully pushing baby Axel in his stroller.

The giggling girls did not hear their mom over the loud music and played a game of tag. Hearing crashing water, curious eyes of passers-by looked up and widened in awe of the sight. Towering at the center of the plaza was a grand fountain that became the pride of the community. This two-tiered, cement landmark was a remarkable sight. The top of this fountain was made of three sculptured giant petals pointing upwards where water jetted up to splash down into the basin below. Below these petals was a tier row of sculptured fleur-de-lis with water also flowing down from them.

Colored lights that were recently added inside the base to illuminate the fountain produced a prism of dancing lights. This truly wondrous sight coupled with the rippling sounds of its flowing water hypnotized passersby.

The north eastern section of the plaza was occupied by several bazaars where the locals sold their goods. Down the aisles, there were displays of plants, clothes, sunglasses, kitchen wares, toys, tin metal works, woodcraft, and crystal goods. There were also activity booths for candle and pottery making, face painting, and soap sculpting. There was even a palm reading booth at the south end section.

The western section inside the plaza housed the thrill rides, Ferris wheel, and carnival games. Naturally, it attracted crowds of interested families and was filled with shrieks of delight. The teens gathered around the carnival games and did their best to shoot targets, knock down cans and bottles, shoot hoops, and win coin-tossing challenges. Winners were presented with coveted stuffed animals while losers were appeased with useless knick-knacks. There were also kiddie rides, like the merry-go-round, little airplanes, and frog-hoppers. Most popular of all were the pony rides; a lengthy line snaked through the crowd as kids waited for their turns to ride the ponies.

String lights hung from one light post to another, brightly illuminating the entire plaza. Between the booths and rides, there was a short pathway leading the south side, to an eatery site. Volunteers prepared a variety of hot and deli sandwiches, pizzas, pies, cakes, chips, dips, and barbecue, which was a crowd favorite. Drinks for young and old alike were free with combination meals. Benches were organized in rows for guests to eat while a brass quartet entertained the crowd with their songs.

The plaza was bustling with activity throughout the day and into the night. Townsfolk and even visitors from neighboring communities arrived as early as eight in the morning. Everyone enjoyed the day, especially the children of the Knight family, Leda, who was five, and Christa, three years old. Meanwhile, Sarah pushed their baby boy, Axel, in a stroller while Charles proudly led his family around the fair.

As they were walking, they stopped at every kiosk looking at the goods for sale. Sarah decided to buy souvenir toys for the kids, while the girls dragged Charles toward the carnival games. Leda and Christa were ecstatic about the giant stuffed animals their dad won for them.

At noon, they headed toward the eatery for a late lunch. Charles bought burgers and fries for all except for Axel, who drank milk. Sarah had to chastise Leda and Christa for shoving fries up their noses and making a mess. When the quartet started to sing, the girls got up and danced around the table, chasing each other and shrieking.

Frustrated with the unruly girls, Charles declared, "It's time to go home."

"But, why?" Leda protested. "Can't we stay a little longer?"

"It's past Axel's naptime, your dad and I are tired, and I think we all need to rest," Sarah explained.

Charles added, "If we stay, we won't come back for the dance, and we'll also miss watching the fireworks."

"Fine," the girls whined, stomping their feet as they petulantly followed their parents out of the plaza.

Since they lived nearby, they decided to exit through the south gate because there was a shortcut trail leading back to their home a couple of yards up the mountain. It was a red brick suburban house with three bedrooms, the master bedroom for Charles and Sarah, another room was for Leda and Christa, and the smallest room was for baby Axel.

As soon as they got home, Sarah laid Axel in the crib, where he instantly fell asleep. Then she checked on the girls and found them both already dozed off. She set the kitchen alarm clock to go off in three hours. Finally, she proceeded to their bedroom, where she found her husband also napping. She was so thankful to finally lay down and rest.

The loud buzzing of the kitchen alarm clock woke them all up. Sarah cleaned Axel and gave him a bottle of milk to keep him calm. Because it was getting dark, Charles decided to drive everyone back to the plaza. The ride was short, and they were lucky to find a parking space close to the north entrance. This time, they headed straight to the party on the south side next to the eateries. This was a quadrangle normally used for outside dining. The tables and chairs were temporarily removed to make room for a dance floor.

Disco lights beamed over the dance floor, where couples were already dancing to the music played by the band composed of six musicians, the quartet with two additional ones playing a guitar and drums. People sat on benches eating, chatting, and having a fun time.

Charles and Sarah sat on the bench next to the buffet table. Christa and Leda walked to the table and grabbed some sandwiches. "I'll get the drinks," Charles announced as he stood to go to the ice coolers.

While they were eating, Sarah elbowed Charles and whispered, "Look who's coming. It's your nosy cousin, Linda. I wonder what gossip she's spreading now."

With a vapid sneer on her face, Linda strutted up to them and said, "Good evening, Charles, Sarah. How've you been?"

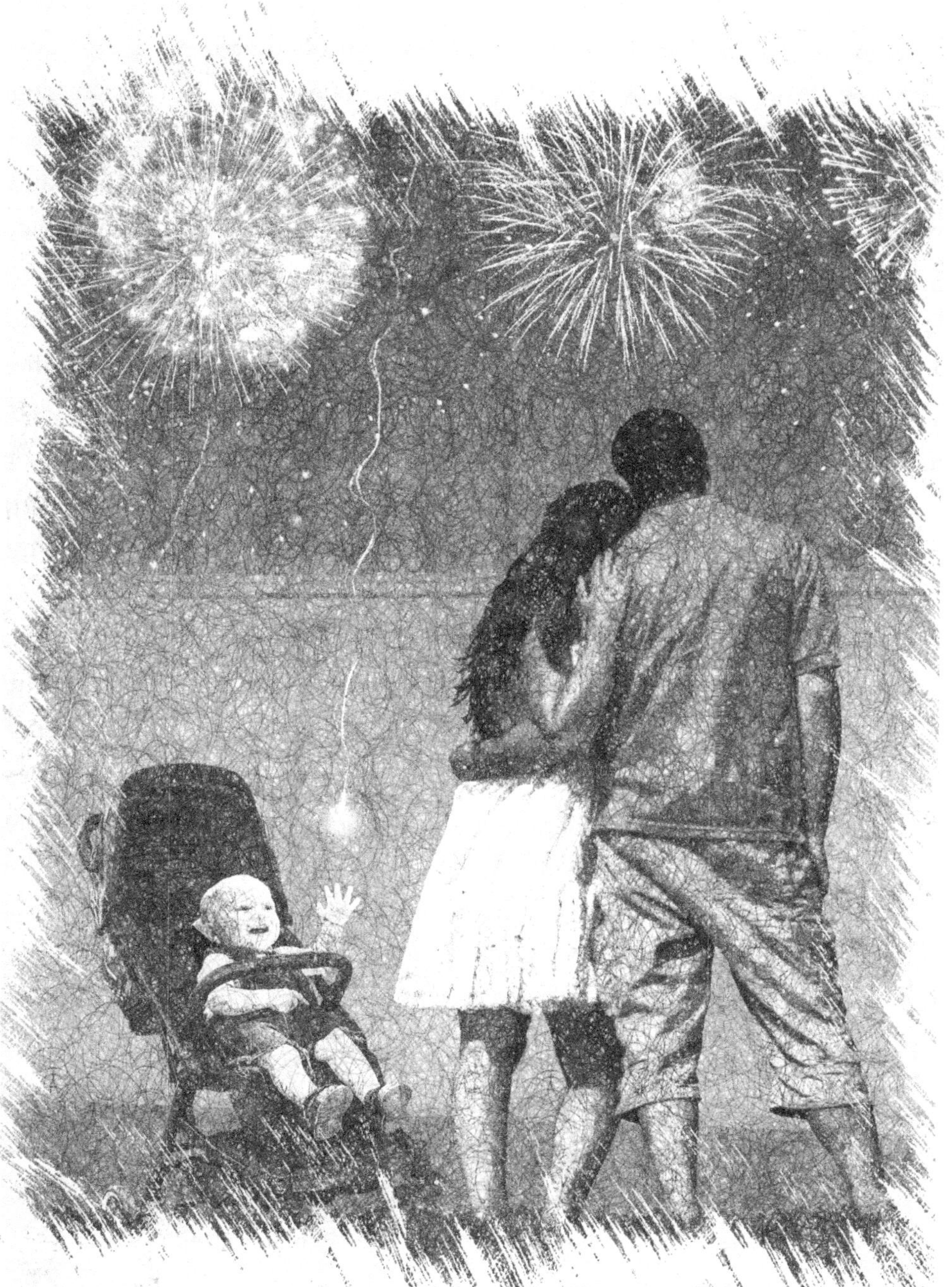

Charles answered, "Never better."

"Well, I heard Doris is leaving her husband because she found out he was having an affair with his secretary," Linda proclaimed.

"Linda, do not believe all those rumors. How's Bill? Is he coming tonight?"

Bill Stone, Linda's husband, was not exactly the ideal, faithful husband either, so as soon as she heard his name, she darted off to another table. Smiling at each other, Charles and Sarah were relieved by her departure.

After eating, Leda and Christa played hide and seek around the area. Two of their cousins, Steve and Adam Curtis, came over to join them for a while. After a few hours, Axel fell asleep in the stroller while the girls napped on their parents' laps.

Just before the stroke of midnight, the host excitedly announced, "Attention everyone, fireworks shall begin in a few minutes!" The dancing stopped, and couples returned to the benches.

The band played a patriotic song, as the fireworks began to burst in the sky. Everyone, even the sleepy kids, looked up to watch them light up the dark night in an array of colors. The band continued playing until the end of the show. People hugged and wished each other a happy new year. Charles and Sarah kissed and hugged both girls. They bent down to kiss Axel, who had just turned one year old. He'd been born at the stroke of midnight.

Just before the fireworks ended, one odd spark drifted down from the sky landed on baby Axel. He wailed loudly and cried incessantly. Charles and Sarah were shocked by the spark burning his right palm. They both panicked and tried to extinguish it with their hands.

When that didn't work, Charles frantically bellowed, "Help! My baby's hand is on fire. Where is Dr. Trent?"

Sarah, thinking quickly, grabbed the extra blanket from the baby bag and used it to wrap Axel's hand, hoping to smother the strange flame.

People started turning to look at Axel and called more loudly for Dr. Trent, who grabbed his medical bag and rushed over to help.

Sarah handed Axel over to him. Dr. Trent removed the blanket and opened Axel's hand, but the spark had now died, and with it, everyone else's interest in the mini drama. As the crowd turned away, Dr. Trent laid Axel on the table. He dabbed burn ointment on Axel's palm and loosely bandaged his tiny hand. With the cooling sensation of the ointment dulling the pain, Axel finally settled down and fell asleep.

The band resumed playing music, and couples slowly moved toward the dance floor again. When the revelries resumed, Charles and Sarah decided to head home. After the initial scare, everything seemed to return to normal, but fate has something else in store for Axel. The wound on his hand would never truly heal, but rather, remain a scar permanently embedded in his hand. How would this tragic incident come to change his life, put him to a diverging path, and lead him to an unknown destiny? That, for now, remained a mystery.

── CHAPTER 2 ──

Waking Up

Thirteen years after that fateful New Year's Eve, the scar caused by a flare from the fireworks still marked Axel's palm. As he grew, the scar didn't seem to fade at all. Even though he was resigned to accepting this as an annoyance, he habitually rubbed his hand as soon as he woke up in the morning, hoping to see nothing but unblemished skin.

Every so often, his scar would burn and send a shooting pain up his arm. When he was little, doctors x-rayed his hand, but they couldn't explain why his hand still ached years after the burn had healed.

Since he still occupied the smallest room in the house, there had been many changes made to it over the years. Charles expanded his room and converted his oak wood crib to a small bunk when he became a toddler. As he grew taller, a wooden-framed twin sized bed was pushed against the wall across from his closet. A unique, ball-shaped lamp and Axel's favorite family photo were set on top of a matching nightstand next to the bed.

Other than the bed, the biggest additions to his room were a desk and a chair that were placed next to the window adjacent to his bed. Whenever he was stressed, he read one of the nineties sci-fi books he kept on the four-shelf bookcase located next to the cabinet that was in an extra space beside the closet. As cramped as his bedroom was, Axel loved this tiny space, as he always felt it was perfect for him.

A few weeks before the end of the year, Axel had started having disturbing dreams that sometimes became nightmares. Two nights before New Year's Eve was one of those nights. He had tossed and turned all night until his mom knocked on his bedroom door. "Wake up, Axel, wake up."

Startled, he instantly sat up and peered through the window. Groaning, he fell back on his pillow and rubbed his eyes. To his dismay, it was still dark outside.

He was only half-awake when his mom pounded on his door. Remnants of events and scenes from his dream swirled in his mind. He remembered being on a seashore and meeting a man wearing a hooded cape. He also saw himself fighting for his life against… someone? There was no clear vision in his mind. These dreams occurred more and more frequently as he grew older. This made him anxious. Axel felt a chill just thinking about them.

Why do I keep having these dreams? Try as hard as he did to remember the details, no other images came to mind. With no answer to this question, he soon fell back asleep.

Moments later, he felt some water sprinkle on him. He wiped his face, thinking he was still dreaming, when another spray of water attacked him. He sat up and saw Christa towering over him. She was still in her flannel pink pajamas and held a spray bottle at his face with a mischievous grin.

At sixteen, she was taller than most of her classmates, naturally athletic, and particularly good at basketball and volleyball. She was allowed to join the varsity teams when she was only a freshman and had caught the eye of college coaches. Now a sophomore, Christa was already a top national prospect after leading the school to the state championships.

Playing tricks on Axel was something she enjoyed doing every chance she got. She took a step closer and sprayed him in the face again.

"Stop it," Axel complained, "What was that for?"

Christa put her free hand on her hip. "You didn't wake up when mom came in here an hour ago."

"It's still dark. Why do I have to get up so early?" Axel protested.

"Mom is already making breakfast and she woke me up to get you out of bed. Didn't dad tell you to go help him in the woods?"

"Right," he mumbled, wiping his face with his pajama sleeves. "But you didn't have to do the water thing. I'm soaked," he whined while Christa walked out of his room with a satisfied look on her face, her "good deed" done for the day.

Axel was five foot four and still shorter than Christa, which annoyed him a lot. He was anticipating the day he would be as tall as her or maybe even taller. He was a good-looking boy, who took after his mom. He was skinny, had dark auburn hair, and brown eyes. Girls liked him but because of his contentious relationship with his sisters, he was always hesitant to be friends with them.

Shaking his irritation as he got out of bed, he collected the clothes he planned to wear and went straight to the bathroom. Thinking of the work ahead, he hoped this day would not be such a drag.

— Chapter 3 —

At the Breakfast Table

Axel groggily dragged himself to the kitchen, where his mom was bustling about preparing a huge breakfast. Sarah was wearing her usual apron with her name embroidered at the center. Her auburn hair was tied in a ponytail that was quickly unraveling, and her dark brown eyes were laser-focused on the task in front of her. Their kitchen was tiny, but with Sarah's organizational skills, every item had a place. This quality, coupled with her baking skills and great customer service, made her bakery very successful.

The first thing that he noticed as he entered the room was the aroma of coffee wafting through the air. He heard the sizzling of bacon frying and eggs cooking while Sarah flipped pancakes on a flat griddle. He was always awed by his mom's cooking skills.

Charles kissed Sarah, "Thanks for making breakfast this early."

"Morning, son," Charles said cheerfully, as he entered the back door. At forty-five years old, Charles still had a boyish charm, and his face was accentuated by a mustache. He had warm, blue eyes and salt and pepper hair. He'd been athletic as a young man, and Christa clearly took after him. He was always a hard worker and a great mechanic. Inheriting his dad's repair shop enormously helped him thrive in the business. Honesty was a trait his father inculcated in him since he first held a tool. With exemplary skills and integrity, he earned his customers' loyalty through the years.

"Help your mom, so we can have breakfast right away. We have a big task ahead of us."

Axel pulled out the plates from the cupboard, the utensils from the drawer and set them all on the table. Coffee was brewing, so he also got the coffee cups, sugar, and milk.

His dad plopped down on a chair, took his thick gloves off, rubbed his hands together, and looked with anticipation at the coming breakfast.

Axel cocked an eyebrow. Being so young, he could not comprehend how his dad could be so happy at the prospect of hard labor. "Dad, we are going to do a lot of physical work in the woods, but I don't know how you can be so cheerful about it."

Instead of explaining, Charles and Sarah made eye contact and laughed heartily.

Axel groaned. "Ugh… I'll never understand grown-ups."

Charles and Sarah laughed some more.

While Sarah laid the pancakes, fried eggs, and bacon on the table, she declared, "I am going grocery shopping today. Does anybody need anything from the store?"

"Would you buy me some chocolates, please?" Axel asked.

"Hey, why do you get to have chocolate?" Leda questioned, as she entered the kitchen.

As the oldest of the three kids, Leda believed she had the right to dictate orders to the younger siblings. She was a senior in high school and was getting ready to graduate. She had become the lead singer for the music club after being found to have a beautiful voice. She was not as tall as Christa, but she had a pretty face, brown eyes, and wavy, black hair. She always wore pink lipstick, at least as often as she could get away with it.

"Well, for one, I get good grades," Axel said proudly. True enough, Axel got excellent marks, usually ranking him first in his class. Being a very smart kid, he helped tutor some of his classmates while he breezed through his own work. This gave him more time to hang out with his friends.

Leda curtly said, "Grades do not count. How about your chores? You're always running away from them, leaving us to pick up after you."

"Now, now, stop bickering and start eating. It is going to be a long day; we have lots of things to do, and tomorrow is our annual village fair." With that order from Sarah, everyone quieted down and started eating.

Leda broke the silence. "Mom, can I go shopping with you?"

"Oh, oh, can I go, too?" pleaded Christa.

Knowing her daughters' propensity for buying more than what they needed, Sarah hesitated.

In unison, they both said, "Please."

"Fine, but make sure you clear off the table and wash the dishes. Also, it is still early, there is still time to clean the house before going out." Sarah said, giving in. "And we are buying only things that we need!"

Leda and Christa grinned at each other and hurried to finish eating breakfast.

While they were talking about shopping, Axel stood and headed out to the truck with his dad.

— Chapter 4 —

The Trip to the Mountain

It was December. The sun was up, but the weather was already very cold. Like his dad, Axel wore a sweatshirt under a thick, blue parka with a pair of gloves and boots to match. He brought his dog, Shushu, and some toys to keep her entertained. Shushu was so excited to join the trip that she could not keep still.

Once the tools were loaded into the cargo box, Charles powered up the engine and turned on the defroster and heater. Shushu sat on Axel's lap inside the truck while Charles scraped the hardened ice off the windshield.

Charles drove out of their driveway and turned left to head up the mountain. He made a sharp right onto a lane that led into the woods then cautiously followed the narrow, zigzagging path.

There were tall pine trees, several young fir trees, and patches of wildflowers along the way. The view amazed Axel; it felt like a serene, wondrous place unaffected by modern civilization. He opened the window to sniff the air. The smell of the pine trees was so refreshing that he closed his eyes and took a few deep breaths. He was still savoring the smell, when Charles slammed on the brakes, causing Axel to jerk forward into his seatbelt then slammed back into the seat.

"Ouch! Why did you do that?"

His dad smiled and pointed to the lane ahead. Blocking the path was a family of seven white ducks crossing the street in a neat line. Their rhythmic movement was synchronized left to right to left, except for the tiniest duck at the end of the line struggling to catch up. Axel held his breath, as the ducks crossed the lane oblivious to the truck that stopped for them. Charles had to wait several minutes for the slow, waddling creatures to pass. When the tiniest duck triumphantly reached the other side, Charles resumed driving, and Axel craned his neck to see if the ducks were okay. He smiled. They were heading for a pond surrounded by lush greenery.

Upon reaching a small clearing, Charles turned sideways to park at the center space.

When Charles parked the truck, Axel broke the silence. "Dad, why do we always chop wood from trees in this place and just how much do we have to get?"

"I think you forgot what I told you before. Your grandpa gave us this land and, luckily, it is densely filled with trees," he replied, getting out of the truck and gathering his tools. "The weatherman said this season would be much colder than last year, so we have to get as much as our truck can hold."

"But... but how long...?" Axel begrudgingly asked, as his anxiety began building at the thought of spending the whole day in the forest, bored with nothing else to do but play with Shushu.

"I think we can get this job done by lunchtime," Charles answered with a wink.

Unsure if it was a joke or if his dad meant it, Axel pouted, following behind him.

Charles carried the chainsaw, and Axel pushed a red wheelbarrow big enough to hold several pieces of chopped wood. Soon his dad said, "Leave that here so that it won't be crushed when a tree falls. You can go back and stay in the truck. I'll call you when I need you to start loading."

"Okay," Axel answered, nodding. As he parked the wheelbarrow, he saw his dad select a particular dead tree to cut. He turned around and ran straight back to the truck. A few minutes later, he heard the loud roar of the chainsaw motor which quickly changed to a high-pitched whine, signaling that Charles had started cutting the tree. The sound was so piercing that Axel and Shushu hurriedly got inside the truck. He closed the windows and put his headphones on. With a sigh of relief, he sank down in the seat to relax. Meanwhile, Shushu, trembling in fear, sought refuge by jumping on Axel's lap. Cuddled together, they fell asleep.

— Chapter 5 —

Return of a Stranger

A short while later, Axel woke up and got out of the truck. With arms stretched, he closed his eyes and took a deep breath, savoring the fresh air. Then he opened the side door for Shushu to get out. The dog gleefully jumped to the ground and ran around the open space. Axel took the frisbee he brought for them to play with and threw the toy into the air. Instinctively, the dog ran and leaped to catch it. Both Axel and Shushu were enjoying the game when suddenly the dog stopped playing and started barking for no apparent reason.

"Hey, Shu, what's wrong?" To calm him down, Axel pulled out a bag from his pocket. "Here, have a treat." Axel patted his head and fed him. Shushu ate the treat but then continued to bark behind Axel. Wondering what was agitating the dog, Axel turned to look back. He was startled to see a bearded old man standing next to the truck. Overwhelmed with fear, he was unable to move and all he could do was look at him from head to foot.

The man wore a black, hooded cape that reached down to his knees. He wore very dark sunglasses and boots that had pointed tips, like... elf shoes? His right hand held a staff that was as tall as him. It was metallic with engravings etched into the upper part of the staff and a crystal gem at the center.

Axel's heart started beating faster, as the old man moved to face him. He tousled Axel's hair and said, "It's been a long time, Axel. Let me look at you. Boy, you did not grow much... still scrawny since I last saw you." He gripped Axel's arms. "I was hoping you would have more muscles after a few years."

"Stop that!" Axel shoved his arm away, took a deep breath, and started backing away. "Who... who are you and how do you know my name?"

The old man snorted and lowered his hood, exposing his long, white hair, which was tied back in a ponytail.

"Don't you remember me, boy? I visited you three years ago on your birthday. I even gave you a gift, something very valuable," the old man replied.

Axel stopped moving and just stared blankly at the old man.

"Oh, for crying out loud, don't tell me that you forgot all about it." The old man's look of worry turned into anger. He stepped forward and grabbed Axel's jacket. "What did you do with it? Did you throw it away?"

"Please don't hurt me. I don't remember. What was it, anyway?"

"That valuable thing is what you call a tapestry. I gave it to you in a special bag."

Axel closed his eyes to think. "Now I remember. I didn't throw it away. It's in my bedroom closet," Axel answered, still shaking in fear. "I also remember you, and you still look as old as when I first saw you."

The old man let go of Axel's jacket and smiled. "Glad to hear you kept it. Good, good, good… then I can tell you what you must do." With this said, the old man's mood changed.

Axel was able to compose himself and stood up straight.

"You are still short. I thought you'd be much taller by now, too," the old man chuckled.

Axel protested, "I did grow taller and look," he flexed his arm, "I have more muscles… and… and stop calling me 'boy.' My name is Axel! I'm gonna be fourteen on my birthday tomorrow."

"Is that so?" said the old man in a low, cynical voice. He moved closer to examine Axel from head to foot and then looked away. "Huh, I suppose you grew up a bit. In any case, I will now tell you what to do with the tapestry. Against my better judgment, you were chosen for this task." The old man twisted his head, looking to his left and right as though to make sure they were alone, then pointed a finger at Axel and sternly said, "Boy, you have a destiny to fulfill, whether you like it or not." He gave Axel a fierce look.

From a distance, Axel heard his dad calling him. Shushu started barking again. He looked at the old man and said, "If you don't mind, I have to go to my dad now."

"Okay, but I won't be far away." He turned then gradually vanished into thin air.

Axel was taken aback by his disappearance. He tried to look around for the old man, but he was nowhere in sight.

His dad called him again. "Axel, come on up."

"I'll be right there," he yelled back. He locked Shushu back inside the truck and returned to where he had parked the wheelbarrow earlier then pushed it to where his dad was. When Axel saw all the pieces of wood that his dad had chopped, he frowned. *Ugh, that's a lot of wood. It will take me forever to finish loading them in the truck.*

Axel began stacking the pieces of wood into the wheelbarrow, and when it was full, he pushed it back to their truck. Thankful that the old man was nowhere in sight, he began to unload the chopped wood and arranged the pieces in rows inside the truck's cargo box.

When he finished emptying his wheelbarrow, he returned to get another load. He was glad his dad was using an axe instead of a chainsaw. It would have been so unbearably loud to be near it. Axel loaded the chopped wood onto his wheelbarrow and returned to the truck again, without incident. This process was repeated several times until half of the truck's cargo box was filled with wood just from the first tree. Axel suspected that their work was not done.

True enough on his last trip, Charles announced that he was going to cut another tree, but a much smaller one this time.

"I thought we were done!" Axel protested.

"Stop complaining. A smaller tree should take less than half the time."

He mumbled a few complaints, but Charles just ignored him and powered up the chainsaw again. Thankful that he had his headphones around his neck, Axel placed them on his ears and immediately parked the wheelbarrow at the same place.

Shushu started barking when he saw Axel walking back. The instant Axel opened the door, Shushu jumped excitedly on him as though he had not seen him in years. Shushu gave so much love and attention to Axel.

They were both enjoying each other's company when, in a flash, the old man reappeared squeezed between Axel and the dog. Axel fell backwards, and Shushu barked angrily.

The old man snorted. "Oops, I miscalculated. I thought you were sitting on the bed of the truck."

"Now, what do you want?" Axel yelled over the chainsaw, no longer afraid of the strange, old man. "By the way, what's your name?"

"My, my... seems like the scared, little boy became a bit braver."

Axel and Shushu moved farther away. "I can't hear you." Axel answered, pointing to his earphones and proceeded to put his dog inside the truck.

The old man sat on the tailgate of the truck and loudly answered. "My name, Ujin. I am the military advisor to the Queen, the ruler of our kingdom. My task is to bring you to our world and, when needed, assist you through your destiny as the Chosen One."

"What kingdom are you from? What destiny are you talking about?" Axel asked.

Ujin sighed. "I know this is quite overwhelming for you, but just do what I tell you to do, and you'll be fine. When you get home, hang that tapestry on the wall. At midnight tonight, stand in front of the tapestry and put your right hand in the center of the circle. Then recite these words: 'I am your humble servant, please let me in.'" Ujin uttered the words softly and with a reverence that took Axel by surprise.

He continued, "If you are really the Chosen One, you will be allowed to enter another dimension, another world... our world."

"Wait a minute; you're from another world? That means you're not human. You're an alien. Geez, this is weird. I don't believe you!" Axel exclaimed. "Even if it's true, why do I have to be your servant? I don't want to be anyone's servant."

"You won't exactly be a servant," Ujin said, rolling his eyes. "I never knew why, but those words translated to your language are the only ones that can open the portal."

Axel gave Ujin a look of doubt. "What do you mean by portal?"

"Portal is a word in your language. Don't you know what it means?" Ujin answered with a questioning look.

"I know what a portal is… it's like a door."

"Well then, why do you still ask for the meaning of portal? Anyway, that portal is the doorway to another dimension. When you place your right hand and say those words, the portal will open, and you will be transported to our world. A word of advice: when you land in our world, you will experience dizziness at first. All you need to do is stay still, and your balance will be restored."

"Why me? Just why do I have to go to your world? You are obviously upset that I'm the so-called Chosen One. I never asked for this. Why can't you or any one in your world fulfill this destiny?" Axel continued to question Ujin. "What about my parents and friends? They would be worried if I went missing. And what about school? I can't miss school."

Ujin sighed with frustration. "Our Queen can tell you why you are the Chosen One. Haven't you ever wondered about the scar on your hand? You see, that is what connects you to my world—that is your destiny. Besides, if you don't fulfill this destiny, your dreams will never give you peace."

"How do you know about my dreams?"

"Oh, I know everything about you. I have been watching you since you were a baby. That is all I can say for now. Don't forget what I told you to do. The tapestry will call you when it's time." With those words, Ujin stood up from the tailgate, turned, and vanished again.

Inside the truck, Shushu had been jumping up and down while the old man was talking to Axel, but calmed down when he disappeared. When the sound of the chainsaw stopped, he went to check on his dad's progress.

Seeing that his dad was almost done, he started loading the chopped wood into the wheelbarrow again. It took fewer trips back and forth to finish the load. Once Axel hauled the last pieces of wood, Charles returned to the truck, set the chainsaw, axe, and wheelbarrow in the truck bed, and wedged a couple pieces of wood behind the loose items to prevent them from slipping.

Axel was so glad to go home. He rubbed his ears to relieve them from the ringing sound of the chainsaw, as Shushu got comfortable in his lap for the ride back home. On the way back, he wondered if what happened was real; if the tapestry was really a door to another world, and if he really had this unbelievable destiny. More than that, he wondered why a simple, scrawny boy like him would be the "Chosen One." And chosen for what? *This is so ridiculous… this can't be true… but then again… maybe!* His mind raced, as he worriedly looked down at his hand.

── Chapter 6 ──

Ladies' Shopping Day

While Axel and his dad were in the woods, Sarah and the girls went shopping in the city. They rode in their big, clunky, red, four-door Oldsmobile car. The rhythmic pattern of engine noises was like sounds produced by instruments in a marching band with no melody. This was Charles and Sarah's first car; it was old but still had sentimental value for them both. Being a mechanic, Charles did the maintenance to keep it in good condition, except for the noise that he was not able to get rid of.

During the ride, Sarah started the conversation. "Girls, don't be so mean to your brother."

"He's annoying, mom. He's such a clumsy nerd. He embarrasses us. We both have an image to uphold in school," answered Leda.

Christa added, "He's lazy, too. He's stubborn, and all he wants to do is read, sleep, or play with his friends. He doesn't help with the chores."

"Still, he's your brother. The best thing you can do is help him be more responsible. Besides, he helps you with your projects and assignments, too. Doesn't he?"

"I guess so," Christa replied.

Leda shrugged. "We'll try, but no promises."

"We're here," Sarah announced. She exited the main road and slowed down as she entered the parking lot. She drove through rows of cars looking for a vacant space that was wide enough for their vehicle. After a few turns, she found an empty one along the outer row not so far from the entrance.

Before she stepped out of the car, she pulled the grocery list from her purse. Leda volunteered to get the fruits and vegetables. Since Sarah was going to bake a lot of pies and cookies to sell at the plaza and to donate to the dance, she decided to get the rest of the groceries with Christa. She tore off the part of the list that had the vegetables and gave it to Leda. Christa wanted to pick up some stuff on her own too, but her mom refused. Sarah ignored her whining. "Let's go, Christa" she ordered.

To Leda, Sarah said, "After you gather all the items on your list, go to cashier number one, and if we are not there, just wait for us. Okay?"

"Sure, mom," Leda said, then walked towards the vegetables and fruits section.

Sarah was scheduled to sell pies at the annual festival and donate some to the dance. For Axel's birthday, Sarah planned to bake Axel's favorite chocolate cake while Charles was to barbecue beef and chicken. Row by row, Sarah and Christa gathered the ingredients to bake the pies and cake. They also picked up the meat and a bag of potatoes.

Christa tried to sneak some items into the cart, but Sarah kept a keen eye on the items her daughter took from the shelves. Other necessities for the girls were placed in the cart. Sarah reluctantly agreed to buy Christa a small eye shadow compact that was on sale.

When they reached the last aisle, Sarah picked up the frozen goods in the last row and proceeded to cashier number one. Seeing that Leda was not there even if she only had to get fruits and vegetables that were in her list, Sarah pulled Christa to look for her sister.

Sarah's intuition was confirmed when from far away, she saw Leda tossing her long hair and flirting with a boy who was stacking vegetables. As she and Christa got closer to the pair, she saw the boy give Leda a kiss. It seemed like a brief kiss, but it still upset Sarah. She took a deep breath and tried to compose herself. Christa saw it too and let out a little chuckle.

Sarah gathered her thoughts and then began to speak. "Leda, I see that you have a friend here at the store. Won't you introduce us?"

Leda was so embarrassed, her face turned red. She was speechless at first, but when she regained her composure, she announced, "Mom, this is Kevin Bell. Kevin, this is my mom, Sarah, and this is Christa."

Sarah extended her hand, "Hi, Kevin."

"It's nice to meet you, ma'am, Christa," said Kevin. Although he was embarrassed, he reached out to shake Sarah's hand. Unfortunately, he was holding lettuce heads in both hands, so he tossed the pair of heads on the stacker, which in turn, dislodged two more heads of lettuce. With his fast reflexes, he jumped into action to catch the runaway heads of lettuce before they hit the floor. Except for one lettuce that got squeezed beneath his chest, he succeeded in saving three at the cost of smashing his face on the floor.

They all tried to control themselves, but the sight was too much for them not to burst out laughing. Leda took the rescued lettuce heads from Kevin's hands so that he could stand up. He removed some of the leaves that were pressed to his apron and wiped his hands on a towel.

"How long have you known each other? Sarah asked

"Kevin went to the same school as us but graduated a year ahead of me. He was also in the drama club," Leda said, proudly brushing her hair to the side.

"Oh, now I remember. You were in some plays Leda was in," Sarah said as she turned to Kevin. "So, what school do you go to now?"

"I'm still at the community college. I want to transfer to the university soon to take up Mechanical Engineering," Kevin answered with a smile, as he continued stacking the lettuce heads.

"That's great. Your parents must be proud of you. Are you going to the fair?"

"I'm not sure. My parents are going, but I work most of the day tomorrow."

"If you are not very tired in the evening, come to the dance. You can taste my apple pie."

"I will try. Thank you, ma'am. Please excuse me, I have more vegetables to stack. It was nice meeting you and Christa."

Sarah said, "Sure, nice to meet you, too."

Leda said smiling, "Bye, Kevin."

"Bye," Kevin answered.

When Kevin left, Christa started teasing Leda. She chanted, "Leda's got a boyfriend, Leda's got a boyfriend."

"Shut up!" Leda snarled at Christa.

"Okay, that's enough. Let's finish our shopping." Sarah turned the cart and proceeded to check out the groceries. With an angry stare at Christa, Leda followed Sarah to the cashier.

They loaded the grocery bags into the trunk of their Oldsmobile. Maybe they were tired, maybe they were hungry, but for whatever reason, all three of them were quiet on the way home.

— CHAPTER 7 —

Remembering

Axel and his dad unloaded the chopped wood from the truck and arranged it inside a large bin in the backyard. Charles carried some pieces into the house and piled them in front of the fireplace. Overall, that big job made Axel so tired. He told his dad he needed to rest at least until lunchtime.

Thankful to being back in his room, he removed his jacket, gloves, and boots and immediately laid down on his bed. However, despite being so tired, he was unable to fall asleep. He tossed and turned over and over until he started daydreaming.

It was three birthdays ago, when Axel received a puppy as a present from his mom and dad. It was a mixed German shepherd brown puppy, only a month old. Axel was thrilled, ecstatic to have a puppy. However, as cute as the puppy was, it constantly yipped whenever he sensed any movement nearby. To stop him from continuously barking, Axel yelled "shoo, shoo." Thus, the dog was named, "Shushu."

Axel and Shushu were playing outside when Sarah called him for lunch. He turned toward the kitchen and yelled "Ok, mom." In that split second, Shushu wandered away, and when Axel spun around, he saw Shushu running toward the mountain.

Axel frantically dashed after the puppy without caring for any danger ahead. All he had in mind was to get his dog back. As he ran, he yelled "Shushu, Shushu, come back. Shushu, come back." Shushu ran and ran until he was nowhere to be seen.

Axel was in tears but continued calling, "Shushu, where are you?" Axel kept looking everywhere when suddenly something appeared in front of him. Axel was disoriented at first. He wiped the tears from his eyes. When his vision cleared, he saw an old man wearing a black hooded cape holding a staff standing in front of him. To his surprise, the man was holding his precious dog in his free hand.

Shushu started to yip again. The old man settled Shushu down, and he jumped onto Axel, gleefully licking his face. He was so happy to see his dog that he forgot about the old man.

The man interrupted the happy reunion. "Well, boy, you should take better care of your dog."

Axel responded thankfully. "Yes, sir, I will!"

"Who gave you the dog?" asked the old man.

"Shushu is my mom and dad's gift to me. It's my birthday today, you know. I'm eleven now."

"Gee... eleven, huh, too young, too, too young," moaned the old man, shaking his head.

"Excuse me, why are you saying I'm too young?" Axel asked. He was still afraid of the old man, and Shushu kept barking at him. "Shu, quiet." Axel patted him a bit.

"Never mind. Here, I also have a present for you," the old man said, as he pulled out a long, black, velvety bag from inside his oversized cape.

Axel stared at the old man's long hair and fingernails.

"What are you staring at?" the old man snapped.

"Nothing," Axel said, looking away from him. "Why do you have a present for me?"

"Why? You asked. I tried to be nice... gave you back your dog... then I'm giving you a present and you say 'why,'" the old man replied.

"I'm sorry... it's 'cause I don't know you. I gather you don't know me either, so why would you give me a present?" Axel answered fearfully.

"Well, you are right to ask me that question. You said today was your birthday. You look like a good boy that I can trust. So, I'm giving you this gift. It's a bag and inside it is something valuable. It's what you would call a tapestry." The old man snorted and then handed him the bag.

Axel frowned. "What's a tapestry?"

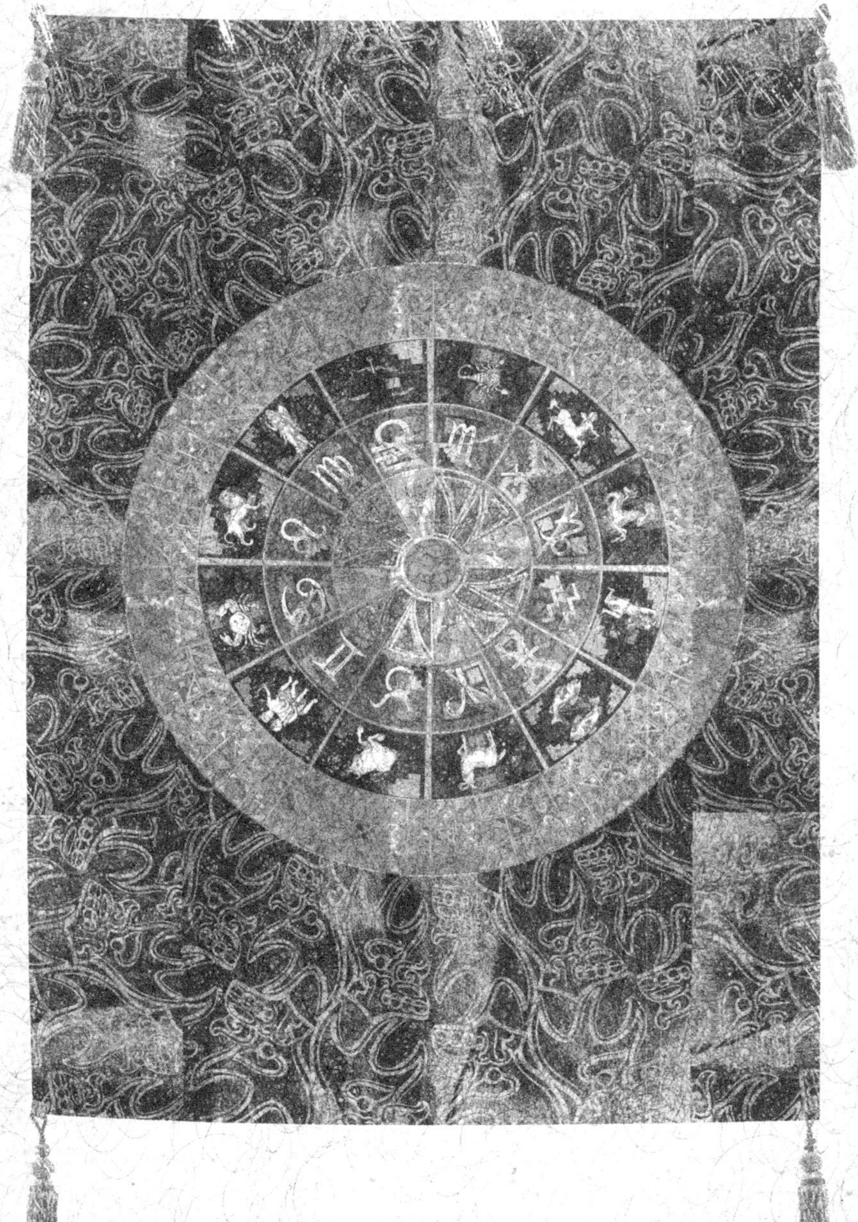

The old man answered, "You'll find out when you open the bag, but not now."

Axel nodded and extended his hand to receive the bag. As soon as he held the bag, he felt warmth in his hand, and a soft glow emitted through the bag. "Why is it glowing? What's happening?" Axel asked and then the glow dissipated.

"My, my, I think it likes you. It glowed because you are the right one to receive this gift. Listen carefully to what I tell you. It's very important that you take exceptionally good care of this gift, even guard it with your life. Never show it to anyone. Keep it until I come back to tell you what to do."

"Why?" asked Axel.

"Because you're it, and if you lose or ruin this, your dreams will never stop haunting you." The old man stared at him so intently that it gave Axel chills. He was so scared all he could do was to nod in agreement.

Suddenly, he heard his mom call for him.

The old man commanded to Axel, "Go now. It is good to meet you, and I will come back to see you again."

Axel started to walk back home, and after two to three steps, he looked back, so he could thank the old man for the gift and finding his dog, but he was nowhere in sight. Axel ran back home carrying Shushu and the bag.

Curious about the old man's gift, Axel went straight to his room, pulled out what was inside the long bag, and slowly unrolled it. Speechless and in awe of the image that unfolded before his eyes, Axel felt transfixed. The tapestry was made of some kind of wool-like material. The image was a circle divided into twelve sections with different multi-colored images within each section. The only image he recognized was the sun at the center of the circle.

Suddenly, Axel shivered, as the memory of the old man's mean stare flashed in his mind. Scared that he would appear from nowhere again, Axel hurriedly rolled up the tapestry, inserted it back into the bag, and then hid it in his closet.

Axel stared at the door of the closet where he had hidden the bag with the tapestry. Now feeling surprisingly rested, he was curious to see the tapestry again. He opened the closet and moved boxes to the floor until he saw the bag, dusty but untouched.

Axel retrieved the bag and untied the knot to open it. As he unrolled it on his bed, he was baffled to see that the tapestry did not have the image he saw before. Thinking that maybe his mind just played tricks on him and that this tapestry was worthless after all, he decided to put it back into the bag. As he started rolling it, to his surprise, images slowly began to appear. These images were as vivid and as beautiful as when he first laid eyes on them.

He also noticed knots at the four corners which he had not seen before. When he loosened them, gold fringes unraveled from each loop.

When the tapestry was revealed in its entirety, the old man's instructions started ringing in his mind. Axel was still not convinced that there was anything magical about this gift, but he decided to play it safe, just in case.

He borrowed his dad's hammer, ladder, and some nails to hang this tapestry on the wall adjacent to the bookshelf. Secrecy was foremost in his mind, so he hung another banner from the ceiling to cover it, although, unbeknownst to him, he was the only one who could see the tapestry.

Shushu was laying down next to Axel's bed looking curiously as his master started hammering, positioning the tapestry, adjusting and then setting it again until it was leveled straight. Satisfied with a job well done, he smiled, jumped on his bed, and fell asleep.

— CHAPTER 8 —

Busy at the Fair

Preparations began the day before the fair in the Knight residence. It went on through the night until seven in the morning, when Sarah finished baking the last four pies. She did not get a full night's sleep, only short, intermittent naps while pies were baking. She made a total of two dozen pies, six cakes and several dozen cookies to sell in the marketplace and donate to the dance. The girls were not thrilled when their dad ordered them to help their mom.

It was Charles's responsibility to load the baked pies, cakes, and cookie boxes into their Oldsmobile, and with Axel helping, they finished fairly quickly. They also packed a folding cart in which to haul the baked goods and a gas grill for customers who preferred warm pies. Sarah made a list of things they needed to bring. Axel was assigned to gather them all.

Leda and Christa took a long time to fix their hair and find the best clothes to wear. Leda chose a knitted sweater over a pink shirt and denim pants. She pulled her hair up in a ponytail and put a ribbon around it. Her finishing touches were some soft make-up and earrings to match her outfit.

Being athletic, Christa was always comfortable wearing T-shirts, denim jeans, and tennis shoes. Although she still preferred to go to the fair with the same style of outfit, this time, she wore a light green sweatshirt with her best jeans.

Charles called out, "Time to go everyone!"

"Almost ready!" Leda and Christa answered in unison.

"Coming," answered Sarah, who had just finished getting ready. "Where's Axel?"

"He's already outside with Shushu," Charles replied.

"Is Shushu coming, too?" she asked as she grabbed the cash box and her purse.

"Of course, did you even doubt it? Was there ever a time when Axel left Shushu behind?" Charles answered with a grin, as they walked toward the front door.

"Leda, Christa, hurry up! And don't forget to bring your thick jackets," Sarah called out to the girls, who both dashed out from their bedroom.

Charles and Sarah got into the car and set out for the plaza. With the car's trunk and back seats filled with boxes of pies, cakes and cookies, Leda, Christa, Axel, and Shushu had no choice but to walk to the village circle through the back road.

When the couple arrived, the plaza was coming to life with the sights and sounds of the fair. Streamers were suspended between stalls around the village circle. Booths were being set up by vendors while food and drinks were brought in for the eatery.

At the gate, Charles paid a rent deposit for one stall and then parked the car on the road closest to the entrance. He unfolded the cart they brought and started loading the boxes in it while waiting for the kids, who arrived several minutes later. They helped load the baked goods into the cart, then pushed it slowly through the entrance toward the fifth booth.

The shelves in the booth were dusty, so Charles wiped each one, then had the girls put down cloth covers. When the entire area was clean, they arranged all the boxes of cookies, pies, and cakes in rows. Christa and Axel went back to the car to get the grill and the rest of the goodies. Sarah set the cash box in a safe corner inside, then helped Charles hang up a sign saying, "Desserts for Sale" at the front of the stall.

The pies smelled so good that villagers who passed by were tempted to buy a box or two. Some of the pies were sold in slices for those who already wanted to eat them.

Leda and Christa smiled at passersby, especially cute boys. Charles saw what they were doing and got upset. He was about to reprimand them when Sarah signaled with her hand to stop him. She shook her head and whispered to him, "Not now. We'll just create a scene."

Charles calmed down and gave her a kiss on the cheek. "What would I ever do without you?"

Sarah just smiled.

Axel tied Shushu's leash to one of the booth's posts and brought him some food and water. As he was feeding Shushu, his friend, Dennis, passed by.

"Hi, Axel, how's it going?" Dennis yelled, making sure to get his attention.

"Oh, it's going. Come over here and play with Shushu and me."

"Sure." Dennis asked his mom's permission and then ran to the stall.

"How long have you been here?"

"Since eight this morning. I've just been playing with Shushu."

"How would you like to play the games in the booths?" Dennis asked.

"Yeah, sure," Axel responded excitedly. "I'll ask my dad first."

He walked toward his dad, who was talking to one of the neighbors. "Excuse me. Dad, can I go to the game booths with Dennis?"

"Okay, but don't forget to be back by lunch. Also, take Shushu with you."

"Thanks, dad." Axel and Dennis, with Shushu in tow, strolled off to the booths. Because the boys had a few coins to spend, they played and enjoyed the usual carnival games, especially the can knocker game. The game booth area was packed with kids, so Axel and Dennis had to pass through the crowd to reach the can knocker booth. They felt anxious waiting in line for their turn, looking at each other, grinning, already feeling competitive. Before they started, Axel tied Shushu to one of booth posts, where he jumped and barked every time the cans dropped down.

When their game ended, Axel untied Shushu and moved away from the crowd. Hearing his stomach rumble, he remembered that his dad said to return to the stall by noon.

He turned to Dennis and smiled. "That was fun, but I gotta go now. See you later."

"Yeah, me too," Dennis replied.

Back at the booth, each of them took turns selling to buyers who came by. They knew most of the customers from their town. A group of kids flocked to their booth wanting cookies for snack. At first, their chaperone did not want to spend money, but the barrage of pleading did not stop until she agreed to buy them treats.

Sarah greeted their chaperone, as she moved toward the counter. "Hi there. I am Sarah. So, you agreed to buy cookies for the kids?"

"Yes, I will get some for them. My name is Grace. My kids here, who are mostly ten years old, are members of the Girl Scouts from the chapter in the next town over. Our cookie sale just finished last week. I promised they could eat whatever didn't sell, but they were so good that there was nothing left, so here I am, buying cookies instead."

"Okay. We have chocolate chip cookies, oatmeal raisin, white chocolate, snickerdoodle, and peanut butter cookies. Which ones would you like to buy?"

"I'll let the kids choose." Grace turned around. "Kids, stand in line, and, one at a time, choose what you want."

When each kid got their share, Grace paid Sarah in cash, guided her group to move on, and waved goodbye to her.

"Thank you for stopping by. Come again."

By noon, more than half of the pies were sold. Inside their booth, there was enough space on the table to set sandwiches and sodas for lunch. Axel arrived just in time. Even Shushu was so hungry, he finished eating his canned food with just a few bites. Leda and Christa started to stand up and leave, but Sarah called them back. "Stop right there. You're not going anywhere until you clean up after yourselves. Oh, and Axel, clean up after Shushu, too."

The girls were disappointed. They had planned to go around the fair after lunch. With frowns on their faces, they threw the trash and cleared out the table.

"Don't give me those looks. Listen, I stayed up most of the night, so you kids have to help. I am exhausted, so I'll just sit here and rest while you continue selling, okay?"

At around three in the afternoon, all the desserts they brought were sold. Sarah was glad she'd left some pies and cookies at home to donate for the dance. She gave some money to each of the kids for their help. They had to clean the stall thoroughly to get their deposit back.

After working and cleaning most of the day, they were all so tired that no one protested about going home. They needed some rest before going to the dance.

— Chapter 9 —

New Year's Eve

The dance had already started when the Knights arrived. They set the pies and cookies that Sarah promised to donate on the food table then looked around for some empty seats. Dr. Trent, who treated Axel's hand when he was a baby, was already dancing with his lovely wife, Sheila. His hair was now all white, and despite his weight gain, he was still as active as ever.

Lynn O'Brien, Charles's cousin, and her husband, Fred, were also present, along with their three kids, who were running around, playing hide and seek between the chairs. Grandma Mary, Sarah's mom, brought her famous fruit cakes that were also set on the table with other dishes, desserts, and drinks.

Charles and Sarah danced to the slow music. Leda was alone, anxiously looking around, while Christa and Axel found their friends. After the band played a few songs, Kevin arrived with his mom, dad, and brother. He immediately approached Leda and gave her a kiss on the cheek.

Charles and Sarah stopped dancing to approach him.

"Good evening, sir, ma'am." He shook hands with the Knights and introduced his parents. "This is my dad, Steve Bell, and this is my mom, Martha. That is my brother, John." After all the greetings, Steve and Martha found seats close to the Knights.

When the next song played, Kevin asked Leda, "Would you like to dance?"

Smiling, she nodded and stood up with Kevin. As they were dancing, Charles and Sarah talked with his parents.

Martha asked, "Is Leda also in college?"

"She is still a senior in high school. I understand Kevin is already in college and working at the same time. You must be very proud of him"

"Yes, we are indeed very proud of him and also of his brother," Martha said. "Leda is very pretty. How many kids do you have?"

"We have three. Leda is the oldest, next is Christa, and our youngest is Axel. Christa and Axel are hanging out with their friends over there." Sarah pointed north to the area where the carnival booths were located.

On the dance floor, Leda and Kevin were eyeing their parents. Leda asked, "Do you think they are talking about us?"

"Probably."

"What do you think they are saying?"

As a slow dance number started, Kevin began to lead and replied, "Tell you what, let's just enjoy the dance and not be worried about them, okay?"

With a sigh, Leda agreed and set her head on his shoulder.

Axel and his friends, Dennis, Stan, and Keith, decided to pass the time by shooting hoops in the basketball court. While the boys were playing, Christa and her friends strolled by on the way to the palm reading booth, chatting about next season's tournaments and gossiping about boys, when Christa noticed Axel. She looked at her friend with a smirk and, on her signal, the girls marched down toward the court.

"Hey Axel. The girls and I have a bet on how fast you would lose against us," Christa said, putting her hands on her waist.

Keith frowned. "Are you sure you want to challenge us?"

"What? Can't handle a little competition?" Christa grabbed the ball, dribbled it down the court, leaped into the air, and dunked it through the hoop with an ostentatious flare.

Keith smiled like a shark and exclaimed, "Game on!"

Knowing how competitive Christa could get with sports, when the game became too intense, Axel stepped off the court and sat on one of the benches. Their game continued until Alfred, the host of the party, signaled the band to stop playing to make an announcement.

"Hello everyone! It's great that you all have come to our fair and joined us on the dance floor, too. I'd like to thank everybody who put this all together, especially the caterers, security, this wonderful band behind me," he motioned toward the band, "and all the wonderful volunteers that helped put up the decorations. It is now fifteen minutes before midnight, and you all know what happens at midnight."

"Fireworks!" everyone cheered.

"That's right. At exactly twelve, the fireworks will begin."

Charles and Sarah looked around. They knew Axel and Christa had wandered off somewhere earlier and hadn't come back yet. Charles turned to Leda and asked her to find her siblings. When she turned around to look for them, she saw that Axel and Christa were already making their way over.

With a big boom, the first firework illuminated the skies. The crowd cheered and clapped. Blast after blast, they continued to explode in different sizes and shapes. Music set the rhythm. Kids watched with wide eyes. Couples stood holding hands. No one ever got tired of this climatic end to the fair.

Immediately after the fireworks ebbed, Alfred yelled, "Happy New Year to all." With that, everyone gave each other their usual hugs.

Then, Alfred added another greeting, "And Happy Birthday to Axel." This was always a special greeting for Axel, who had a dramatic birth on New Year's Eve and a traumatic first birthday. People turned around to greet him, too. Charles and Sarah gave Axel a hug, so did Leda, Christa, Grandma Mary, other relatives, and friends.

Everyone enjoyed the celebration, especially Axel, who got lots of gifts. New Year's Eve was his favorite occasion. He was all smiles until suddenly, his right hand started to throb in pain. Shock and disbelief overpowered him at the sight of the glow emanating from the scar on his palm. He instinctively slid his hand into his pocket.

The crowd in the village circle started to disperse in several directions. The folks who were still full of energy returned to the dance floor when the band resumed playing music. Some hunted for leftover food while families like the Knights decided to go home.

Leda was saddened to separate from Kevin, and Christa suddenly got a headache and wanted to go home. Because Axel still felt the warmth from his right hand, he knew that it was still glowing. He put on his gloves and turned around to stack all his gifts into a plastic bag he found at the food table. Despite its heaviness, he shoved the bag over his shoulder and used his left hand to carry it.

"Hurry up, Axel," called his dad.

"Coming," he answered, as he tried to catch up. Assured that no one saw what happened, he hid his right hand until he got home.

Chapter 10

Axel's First Trip

Back in his room, Axel took his shaking hand out of his pocket and stared at it. The glow emanating from his palm got bigger and brighter. Startled and unsure of what he was seeing, he turned on his light to make sure this was truly happening. Dread chilled his blood, and his heart started to beat faster. This had never happened to his hand before.

He began to panic. Unable to stand, he sank to the edge of his bed, clutching his chest, struggling to breathe. Just as darkness started to cloud his vision, what sounded like an angry voice came from near the window.

"What took you so long?"

Axel was so startled that he fell off the bed. He saw the hooded old man, Ujin, sitting in a lotus position. What was weird was that he was not sitting on a chair. He was just floating two feet above the ground.

Despite his racing heart, Axel managed to pick himself off the floor and return to bed. He took deep breaths to calm his nerves and cleared his throat. "You scared me half to death. Why... why are you here?"

Ujin lowered his body to the ground, stretched out his legs and stood up with the help of his staff. "It's past midnight, where have you been? This moment is very crucial. It is time."

"What do you mean 'it is time'? What time are you talking about?"

"It is time for you to go to Zycodia."

Axel eyed his pillow, suddenly wanting nothing more than to sleep, but instead sighed and asked, "What and where is Zycodia?"

"It is my home world. The portal is closing. You must go now."

"Wait a minute. My mom and dad will be worried if I'm not here. How long do I have to be there?"

"I said you must go. The portal will be closing in less than a minute. I'll explain when we get there. Place your palm on the center of the tapestry."

Axel protested, "No! I'm not going anywhere with you until you explain what's going on."

Ujin pulled Axel from the bed, grabbed his hand, and placed it on the tapestry. The glow from his hand seemed to ignite the circle at the center of the tapestry. Scared of what was happening, Axel tried to pull his hand away, but even with all the energy he expended, his effort was futile.

What happened next was unfathomable, unbelievable. The tapestry started waving and transformed into an unstable field. This was the portal Ujin was talking about. It continued to grow until it matched his size and then suddenly sucked him in like a vacuum cleaner.

"No!" Axel yelled, as he was transported through a tunnel, feeling like he was floating in the sky. It seemed like it would go on forever, but after about a minute, he saw a ray of light. He prayed that it was the exit. Indeed, it was. Upon reaching the exit, he was pushed out and landed flat on the ground with a thump, his face halfway buried in what felt like hot, beach sand.

Slowly raising his head, he shook the grains off his face, spit out some of the sand that had gotten into his mouth, then wiped his eyes to clear his vision. He looked around to see if the tunnel he fell out of was still there. To his dismay, it was nowhere in sight.

What he saw was a seashore that stretched out as far as the eyes could see. Weird, he thought, because the sand was green. The waves that seemed to come from the horizon and broke on the shore were... again, weird. Both the sky and the water were a strange, reddish color.

"Oh no, oh no, oh no—what is this place?" Scared and exhausted, he laid on his back. The warm sand soothed his achy body. He closed his eyes, intending to open them in just a few seconds, but he lost consciousness instead.

When he woke up, he opened his eyes slowly, praying that what happened to him was just a very bad dream and that he was still at home.

Afraid that he was not in his room, he opened his eyes very, very slowly. To his dismay, he was still in the same spot where he landed after exiting the portal. The sky and the ocean were still red. The sand was still green.

As he struggled to stand on his wobbly legs, he noticed what seemed to be a giant crab. Worse, it was charging towards him. With his heart pounding and adrenaline kicking in, Axel turned to dash away. Running through sand was so difficult that he stumbled after a few strides. He stood up to try again but kept stumbling forward until the sea creature caught up to him.

"No! Go away!" he screamed, kicking and thrashing to protect himself. Despite all his strength, the crab clamped its claw over Axel's arms. Axel tried to wriggle out of its claws, but the crab wouldn't let him go. "Why is this happening to me? What did I do to deserve this?" He shouted with tears dripping from his eyes.

"Riqui, stop it! Release him, now!" a thundering voice shouted at the crab.

Axel looked up and saw a tall man with shoulder-length black hair. He was wearing a black cape and holding a silver staff.

"Move away from him," the man commanded.

Axel saw that the crab understood the command. It released Axel from its grip, then moved away and sat down. Strange, seeing the crab sit down in an upright position and fold its claws. Somehow, the crab seemed to be sulking.

Axel turned toward the man. "Who are you?"

"Don't you recognize me, Axel?"

Axel stood up, moved closer, and stared analyzing his face. With some recognition, he asked timidly, "Ujin? Is that you?"

He answered, smiling, "Yep. It's me."

"B-but y-you're not... OLD!" Axel exclaimed.

Ujin cleared his throat. "Nevermind that. You are now in our home world. I wanted to give you a nice welcome, but we cannot stay here longer. Her Majesty is waiting for us."

"This is your kingdom? Where? I can only see miles and miles of nothing."

"Oh, that's right, I forgot." Ujin waved his staff in the air and pressed his hand on Axel's forehead. "Behold, our majestic world!"

Just like the magic in movies, the deserted land and red-colored open space transformed into a breathtaking scenery with mountains, trees, waterfalls, and flowers everywhere. There were birds in the air, strange-looking but still birds. To witness this transformation, especially the slowly changing color of the ocean and sky from red to clear blue, was an indescribable feeling.

Axel's eyes widened in awe.

"Impressed?"

"Yeah, but how is this possible?" Axel asked, rotating to look at the entire panoramic view.

"Well, this is possible with our queen's power. What you saw before is the scene outsiders can see. She created this camouflage as protection against those who have intentions of harming our kingdom. I unblocked the optical illusion in your mind. That is how you are now able to see our world in its true nature."

Axel continued, "So, I got here. Can I go back home now?"

Ujin ignored his whining. "First things first, we need to go to the castle. Things will be clearer for you when we get there." Ujin waved his staff again, and something that looked like a small plane or rocket ship floating one foot above the ground appeared in front of them.

"What is this?"

"I thought you were supposed to be super smart. This is my Swifty, what you would call a jet in your world, but as you can see, it's much smaller. This is our means of transportation, a common vehicle, although not everyone owns one."

The jet was cylindrical, had a pointed nose, and seemed to be made of some sort of metal or glass. There were no windows or tires. The rear was fitted with three guide fins on the rim of the outer covering.

The top canopy opened when Ujin tapped it with his hand. Axel moved closer to peep in. There were only two velvety seats inside. Nothing else was visible.

Suddenly, the crab stood up and cried out, "What about me? I thought you needed me for the mission."

Axel nudged Ujin's arm and whispered, "The crab is talking. The crab is talking!"

Frustrated, Ujin glared at him and said, "I know that."

Ujin turned to the crab and said, "You do have a very important mission to fulfill, Riqui. I will call you when the time comes."

"Fine," the crab answered as it transformed into a human-like form. Axel was surprised to see that Riqui looked like a normal man. As he sulked and turned to leave, he looked at Ujin. "Call me right away. I can't wait." He turned to Axel and smiled. "Also, it's nice to meet you! See you soon."

Axel's stare was still fixated on the crab's transformation when Ujin nudged him to get in the vehicle. Upon entering the Swifty, Ujin took the front seat and Axel sat behind him. The engine came alive and started whirring. A glass dashboard appeared with flashing lights and then a transparent helmet projected forward. Ujin picked it up and placed it on his head. Another helmet emerged in front of Axel's seat.

Axel marveled at the vehicle. He never saw anything like this in his life. The jet was completely see-through, from top to bottom and from side to side.

Ujin grinned. "You have a three-hundred-and-sixty-degree view of the outside, and yet anyone out there would be unable to see anything inside. The surface of the vehicle reflects the surroundings, making it impossible for outsiders to see us. That's the beauty of my trusty friend," he said proudly, as he tapped the dashboard. "This jet has the capability of being camouflaged with the surroundings, like a chameleon."

Thinking back to the beach, Axel understood what Ujin meant. He looked around again and asked, "But if nobody can see other jets, how do you keep from crashing into each other?"

"Now that is a good question," Ujin nodded approvingly.

"Thanks," Axel said, as he patted the side of the jet. To his surprise, a belt projected out and wrapped around Axel's waist. "So, are you going to answer it?"

Ujin chuckled. "Okay. You do know that the shortest route is a straight line, right?"

Axel nodded again, but this time, he was starting to get anxious. "Yeah, but how does that answer the question?"

Ujin pressed a button on the lit-up dashboard. "All vehicles are equipped with sensors that send out signals to alert drivers that they may be in their pathway. That is how crashes are prevented."

Swifty lifted about six feet off the ground and bolted forward. With unbelievable speed, the jet zoomed through space and into the thick forest, catapulting Axel backwards. He covered his eyes and screamed. Mastering his courage, he slowly opened his eyes and straightened himself in his seat. Axel noticed that the direction of the vehicle followed the movement of Ujin's head and hands. He held his breath until they reached a clearing, and, as the jet slowed down, he exhaled a sigh of relief.

Upon reaching a huge mountain, the jet came to a halt and hovered, as two big boulders in front of them began to open like sliding doors in department stores. They glided slowly through the rocks and entered the mountain.

Axel felt his jaw drop but couldn't help himself; this was impressive. *A castle inside a mountain. Unreal… but then again… also awesome.*

— CHAPTER 11 —

Entering the Castle

As the jet passed through the boulder entrance, it careened through a downward passageway leading to what seemed like a parking garage for all sorts of vehicles, lots and lots of them. Looking around, he thought there may be thousands of those things.

Ujin skillfully maneuvered to park his jet in what Axel thought was his personal parking space because the ground had a symbol that he had not seen before. In fact, each lot had symbols that looked a lot like the markings on his tapestry

The jet lowered to the ground, and Ujin touched the dashboard again, powering the engine down. Axel was startled when the roof above them opened, letting a gush of wind blow his hair up.

As scared as he was, Axel wanted to show a brave face. However, his body had other ideas. For one, his legs kept shaking. He leaned on Ujin's back seat as he stepped out of the vehicle. He was still trying to get his balance when Ujin said, "Come on. Let's go."

Axel struggled to follow Ujin. They headed toward a circular structure which was close to his parking space. Axel said, "Let me guess, that's an elevator!"

"Very astute." Ujin remarked and continued walking. When he pressed a button that was on a brace around his arm, a metallic door and an inner glass door started to open, sliding in a circular motion. The floor of the structure began to light up the space inside.

Ujin entered the glass capsule and signaled Axel to stand next to him. Axel was so entranced by the bright floor that he did not see Ujin motion to him.

"Axel!" Ujin yelled. "Get in here."

Startled, Axel obeyed, stepped in, and turned around to view the entire area again. Only then did he notice that there were several of those cylindrical structures everywhere.

When the door closed, they were instantly hurled straight up which made Axel dizzy. "Geez, Ujin, does everything here move at super speed?"

Ujin looked at him and said, "All the new things you have just seen, like my Swifty and these vertical capsules that travel at super speed, are some of our modern inventions. At first, these were stairs like the ones you have on earth. Then, with innovations, they were converted to moving stairs until our mechanical experts and scientists were able to convert them into these capsules that are much faster. One day, I might show you how they work and even how you can use them."

"Wait, what... what do you mean how I can use them one day?" Axel asked.

Ujin smiled. "You are special to our world. I don't see why not."

The capsule jerked to a stop, and the circular glass and the metallic door outside opened. As they stepped out, it descended, leaving an opening in the floor which automatically closed. Axel looked around to check the surroundings. It was empty, like a large landing space. He noticed several huge doors, actually, twelve of them, set in a circle around the area.

The doors, which had arched tops, were very tall. Axel estimated they were maybe double his height. There were no names on the doors, just symbols. Axel had no idea what all those symbols meant, but then again, he remembered they looked like the symbols on his tapestry. They were also the same symbols he kept seeing in his dreams.

"What is this place?" Axel asked.

"This is the fifth level: there are twelve rooms with symbols on every door. They represent the twelve main tribes of our kingdom. These rooms are used for meetings to discuss problems, hold ceremonies, and to even keep books and historical artifacts." Ujin glanced at Axel. "When the right time comes, I will show you each room. We have more important things to do right now. Let's go. We will use the capsule again soon, but I want to show you another way to go up."

They started walking toward an opening in one section of the wall that led to a hallway. They continued along this path until they reached its end. At the junction, there was a ramp that split into two: the left side went up, and the right side went down. Ujin signaled Axel to follow him to the left. He pressed a button on the wall, and a horizontal, foot-long narrow platform projected out of the ramp. They stepped onto it and began to ascend.

As they were going up, Axel was in awe of the breathtaking scenery outside the mountain. Ujin noticed Axel's fascination. "This is like a one-way mirror. We can see outside, but nothing inside can be seen from out there.

"Just like your jet, right?"

Ujin nodded.

Continuing upwards, Axel noticed the crystal-like lights that hung from each side of the ceiling. They dimly lit up the hallway. To his amazement, as they passed through, the lights grew brighter, illuminating the decorative sculpture art on the left side of the wall. He was captivated by the beautiful artwork when he noticed that the lights grew dimmer behind them. His conclusion was that these lights were sensor lights, much like those used on earth.

Axel felt this ramp circle behind the rooms. They went higher and higher until they reached a door at the end. Ujin turned to him and said, "No one unauthorized can pass through this door."

"Will I be allowed?" Axel asked quietly.

"Why do you even ask? You are the reason we are here now," Ujin answered with a smile, as he patted Axel's back.

— CHAPTER 12 —

Axel Meets the Queen

Ujin unlocked the door, not with a key but by placing his hand on a glass panel. Axel thought they were entering a room, but to his dismay, the door opened to the continuation of the ramp on which they had to walk this time.

Axel did not want to walk, but Ujin ignored his whining and kept going, so Axel had no choice but to follow him. In a few minutes, they faced another door. It was also a huge, arched door, but unlike the other doors, Axel recognized the symbol on it as a crown. Like the previous door, it did not have a knob, only a glass panel.

"This is the highest level, and we are going to enter the queen's chambers. It's time for you to meet her majesty, Queen Elyjanah, so behave yourself," Ujin said in a commanding manner.

He pressed a button on the glass panel.

A female voice answered, "Come in, Ujin."

He placed his hand on the panel and the door opened. Ujin bowed and said, "Greetings, your Majesty."

She nodded in response. "Who do we have here? Ahh, let me guess, are you Axel?"

Axel followed Ujin's cue and bowed. "Yes, your Majesty, I'm Axel."

"My, my, I imagined you would look a little older."

"I'm already fourteen. I am still a freshman, that's first year in high school but if I maintain my high grades and pass a special test, I can skip second year and be promoted to third year, a junior in high school.

"Is that so, young man?"

"Um, um, yeah." Axel said. "You don't look like a queen yourself."

Ujin snapped, "Don't be disrespectful."

"Oh, Ujin, that's alright."

Looking at Axel, she said, "Why do you say I don't look like a queen?"

"Well, you've got short hair, and aren't queens supposed to be wearing some kind of long gown with a crown or something?" He hesitated but continued. "You're wearing a shirt and pants."

"You mean I should look like this!" With the wave of her hand from the top of her head downward, she transformed into an elegant lady with long black hair. Her clothes changed from the ordinary shirt and pants to a long, magnificent gown, and a golden crown appeared on her head.

"Gee, do all of you in this world just wave your hand and change anything you want to change?"

"Not everyone has that ability, and those who possess it use it only when necessary. By the way, this is how I really look, but I knew you were coming today, so I wanted to look more casual."

She transformed back to her comfortable outfit. "Are you hungry?"

Embarrassed by the audible growl coming from his stomach, he said shyly, "Yeah, sure. With all that has happened, I kinda don't remember when I last ate."

"Ujin, have Johan bring us some food."

"Yes, your majesty." He bowed and then stepped out of the chamber.

The queen led Axel to what seemed like a dining area. "Have a seat."

Axel sat down on one of the velvet-covered chairs with beautifully sculpted frames. The table was made of glass resting on legs that matched the design of the chairs. The walls of the room had paintings of different sceneries. The queen noticed Axel looking at them and explained that those were scenes from different tribes around the kingdom.

"Tell me about yourself, Axel. Ujin has watched over you since you were a baby, but I'd like to know more about you and what's happening in your life. Tell me about your family and friends."

"My dad, Charles, is a mechanic and has a repair shop that he inherited from my grandfather; he fixes cars and just about anything that is broken. My mom's name is Sarah, and she is a great cook. She loves to bake and owns a small bakery in the village. I have two sisters older than me, Leda and Christa. They're always annoying and mean to me especially Christa, but when I'm in real trouble they help me out."

"You seem like you have a great family. You said that you are going to be a junior in high school. You must be a pretty smart kid to be promoted above your age group."

"So, they say, but it's not always a good thing. Other kids call me names or sometimes try to be friends with me only because they think I'll help them with schoolwork."

The door opened. Ujin, Johan, and three other guys who were wearing white shirts and white hats entered carrying covered, silver platters, which they set on the table. They then returned with drinks and trays of fruit. Johan was a great chef but notoriously klutzy, so he did not carry anything. His clumsiness was always evident when there was a special occasion. Serving the queen and her guests was just such an event. Being aware of his problem, his assistants were always ready for any disaster.

Johan led the way to the table. In his excitement, he tripped over the edge of the rug. His assistants instinctively moved out of the way to protect the food they were carrying. Johan was embarrassed, but he immediately stood up and clapped his hands as a signal for them to set the table.

The queen and Ujin concealed their laughter, but a chuckle escaped from Axel. He covered his mouth and hoped no one noticed.

There were four platters placed on the table, but there were only three people who were there. Axel wondered who else was coming in to join them. He wanted to ask 'why four' but before he opened his mouth, there was a knock on the door.

"Come in," the queen said.

A girl about Axel's age entered the room, kissed Queen Elyjanah, and took the empty seat. Her long, black hair was braided. She was also wearing a T-shirt and jeans. Axel could not take his eyes away from her face. She was pretty and had big, beautiful eyes.

The queen cleared her throat. "Isyna, this is Axel. Axel, this is my daughter."

"Nice to meet you, Axel," Isyna said, smiling at him.

Johan signaled Milo, Troy, and the youngest, Elery, to uncover the platters and pour the drinks. Johan was about to uncover Ujin's, but he blocked his hand and lifted the cover himself. As the covers were raised, Axel was surprised to see that they were being served hamburgers, fries, and personal pizzas.

"You look surprised, Axel. Don't you like the meal prepared?"

"No, no. I love burgers and fries, and pizza too. I just didn't think you'd be eating same food we eat."

"Good. Then let's start."

At first, Axel was shy and embarrassed to eat but when the queen signaled for them to begin, he picked up his burger and took his first bite. It tasted so good. He was very hungry. He could not stop eating until he had cleared his platter.

The queen was amazed. "I'm glad you are enjoying the meal."

"It is good, but how—"

Queen Elyjanah finished the question for him. "How can we have the same food as your world? Well, we have our own dishes, of course, but because you were coming, I wanted you to feel at home. Since you were born, Ujin has been traveling to your world and learning your customs, traditions, language, and food, everything there is to know about your world. That's how we knew what dish you would like to eat. That's how we learned to speak your language, too."

Johan and his assistants cleared the table when everyone was done eating. Queen Elyjanah complimented Johan and his assistants on the hearty meal. They bowed and left the chamber with Johan just holding the empty pitcher.

"Now that we have finished our meal, let's talk about why you are here, Axel. I'm sure you have many questions in mind.

Before the queen began, Isyna, who had mostly been quiet during the meal, said, "Mother, do I have to stay here for the rest of this talk?"

"You may go, Isyna. Thank you for joining our meal."

She stood up, bowed, and left the room.

Axel thought that she was cold, aloof, and a snob. He also couldn't care less about her. Even if she was pretty with big, beautiful eyes.

— Chapter 13 —

Revelations

The queen stood up and gestured for them to move to her study. As Axel entered the room, the huge, floor-to-ceiling bookcase propped against a wall immediately caught his eye. He was so intrigued by the shelves filled with books that he tried to read the titles on the spines. Unfortunately, he could not read any of those characters. To the left and right sides of the bookcase, two magnificent paintings hung from the wall. What they meant was unknown to Axel. As he continued to look around, he was captivated by the glistening chandelier hanging from the ceiling that gave off a glowing warmth above the desk at the center of the room. Queen Elyjanah sat on an elegant, high-backed chair behind the desk and motioned for Axel to sit down on the chair in front of her. He sank into the soft cushion of the lush chair. He liked the comfort of this seat but also felt uneasy, as he had never sat on such a luxurious chair.

Ujin, who was standing next to Axel, bent down to set a small gadget on the middle of the desk. Axel watched closely as Ujin pressed one of the buttons on this object, which instantly lit up and projected an image upward. As he started to speak, he allowed the projection to slowly turn around for Axel to view the three-dimensional image of the country.

"This is the entire world of Zycodia. This image shows the twelve sections that comprise the twelve tribes of the land, just like the countries you have on earth. Know that there are several clans within each tribe which you will encounter as you travel through our kingdom. Notice the symbols shown in every section," Ujin paused, pointing them out. "Each tribe is represented by a symbol that they hold dear, just like the flags that represent each of your countries. Do you recognize the symbols?"

Axel nodded. "Like the symbols on the twelve doors."

Ujin smiled. "Good, seems like you are catching on. Each tribe has a celestial gem they hold as their treasure. By royal decree, the leaders of the ruling clan are ordered to protect their gem because it is the tribe's essence, imbued with powers that keep balance, security, peace, and harmony throughout our world. Through the centuries, tribal rulers invented different, unique ways to protect their gems. It is their deep-seated belief that without the celestial gem, their tribe would be ruined."

"One of the gems was stolen three years ago, and we believed it to have been perpetrated by a subversive group. Luckily, we retrieved it in time; unfortunately, it cost many lives. That prompted Her Majesty to send me to earth to deliver the tapestry to you. Ideally, we wanted you to come to Zycodia as an adult, however, another gem was stolen, and that compelled us to accelerate bringing you here. The balance of our kingdom has already shifted from the first time a gem was stolen. We believe all celestial gems are now at risk."

With his head starting to spin, Axel attempted to speak but could not find the words to express the turbulent thoughts racing through his mind—thoughts trying to figure out how he fits into these troubled times. Feeling his turmoil, the queen stood up, turned, and looked out the window. She returned to her seat and gave Axel a stern look. This look abruptly brought him back to his senses. He anxiously gazed at her, as she took over the conversation.

"I believe that an evil sorcerer named Sevion is behind all these happenings. He considers himself to be the rightful ruler of our kingdom and intends to usurp my crown."

"Fifteen years ago, he plotted to assassinate my father, King Loxin, who was also his brother, by poisoning him. This plot was discovered a moment too late, and the king ingested some of the poisoned food. He collapsed, and royal healers were speedily summoned to save my father. Confessions by a few witnesses pointed to Sevion as the perpetrator. Because he was the king's brother, Sevion was exiled from the kingdom to the Outer Realm of our world instead of being executed."

"By divine grace, my father survived, however his health slowly deteriorated. He battled the effects of the poison but eventually, after a year, he succumbed to death. It was then that I ascended as the Queen of Zycodia."

Axel saw a momentary look of sadness on her face that was immediately replaced by a piercing gaze. Axel felt as though she was peering into his soul. He felt uneasy until she looked away.

"You must be perplexed by your supposed role in all of this."

Axel nodded.

The queen continued, "To understand this, you must know more about our kingdom, our history. Most Zycodians are shapeshifters able to transform at will depending on the tribe they belong to. We have had the ability to travel to other worlds, such as Earth, through worm holes for a certain amount of time. Before embarking on a journey outside our kingdom, travelers are warned that staying in other worlds beyond a certain time limit will prevent them from returning home. They will remain in that world in either human or animal form."

Axel was utterly surprised. "Really? Is that how some animals on earth came to be? Do you know how many Zycodians are on earth? If they remain as animals, will they retain memories of their previous life? Will they forever be stuck on earth or any other world they traveled to?"

As Axel kept rambling on, a servant was called to bring water for the queen to relieve her thirst. She waited for him to exhaust his store of questions.

His raised shoulders dropped and with a sigh, he concluded, "I suppose I cannot look at animals the same way again."

Queen Elyjanah nodded. "When I was much younger, my father told me about one of our ancestors, a warrior-king named Mitron, who traveled to earth after his queen died. He had a taste for adventure and repeatedly journeyed to earth. In one of his travels, he met a female Earthling, and they fell in love with each other. Their love was so strong that he decided to give the crown to his son. Mitron bade farewell to Zycodia to live on earth with his new bride. Eventually, they had a daughter, who became a mother to another daughter. Through generations of female offspring, one descendant would bear the prophesied son."

Axel began to piece it together with a sinking feeling in his stomach.

"That mother, Sarah, gave birth to you, Axel. You are the first male heir of Mitron's lineage on earth and the son of that prophesy."

Being so overwhelmed with all this information, Axel broke out in a cold sweat. Innumerable questions still swirled around his head. He looked at the queen and realized she must have been waiting for a response. "That cannot be right, there must be a mistake. I am just a kid from a small town. I cannot be an alien or even half-alien." His thoughts jumbled, as he continued to babble. "Even if, somehow, this was true—wait a minute, would that mean you could be my aunt or cousin? Anyways, what can I do...? I don't have any magic, and I can't shape-shift. Isn't there anyone here who can fulfill this destiny?"

The queen's face softened when she saw the emotional turmoil in his face, "I apologize, my young kin, that this enormous task has fallen on you at an early age. We would have waited for you to be old enough before travelling to our world, but forces have come into play that compelled us to summon you sooner than we expected. Our world is in danger, and we need you to help. We will grant you all the resources at the Crown's disposal to aide and guide you through this destiny."

The servant returned with glasses of drinks for Axel and Ujin.

With a sympathetic look, the queen said, "Axel, stay here for a while. Try to relax and let this all-information sink in. For now, I have other tasks to attend to, so I leave you with Ujin. When you are ready, he can give you the castle tour."

Axel and Ujin stood up and bowed as she left the study.

— Chapter 14 —

The Castle Tour

After finishing his drink, Axel seemed more relaxed. "If you are ready, we can proceed with your tour of the castle," Ujin said.

Axel nodded and followed Ujin, as he entered a well-lit room. At the center, there was a round, marble-like table surrounded by a large semi-circular velvety blue couch with white pillows. Across from the couch, there were four matching, elegant chairs. The wall had a mosaic painting of the view Axel saw when they were going up the ramp. Ujin went to the corner opposite the queen's chamber door, and with the wave of his hand, a round opening in the floor lit up, and a capsule emerged. The sliding metallic and inner glass doors opened, and as soon as they entered, the capsule closed behind them. Before Axel could catch his breath, they plummeted down at super speed.

When it halted, they stepped into a dimly lit hall. Standing in front of two huge heavy metal doors were two armed guards in uniform outfits. In front of each door was a wheel with twelve symbols etched along the circumference, much like the ones Axel had seen in various places.

"Now, where are we?" Axel asked.

Ujin proceeded to the door, pressed the symbols in a sequential pattern on a panel and placed his hand on it. Then, he turned the wheel two times to the right and two times to the left to unlock it. He then raised the lever located at the right side of the door.

Ujin proudly said, "This is our armory, which is just one floor above the parking level. We store most of our weapons here, but there are smaller storages in every tribal location." As he opened the door, the lights turned on.

"Wow, I've never seen any place like this before." His eyes widened, looking all around the huge storage room that was filled with rows and rows of different kinds of things. He thought, since Ujin said this place was the armory, maybe these things were really weapons.

"Let's start here." Ujin led Axel to the left side of the room. He picked up a weapon at the end of the row. "This is what we call panhâs. They are like the crossbows in your world but not as simple. So that you won't get confused, we'll call it 'crossbow' for now."

"Can you show me how this works? Axel asked.

Ujin picked up a bow and a glass-like container with ten pins that were about twelve inches in length. Each pin was as thick as a pencil and had a pointed tip. He inserted it into a chamber through the front end of the weapon. As he pulled a knob located at the right side, the string above the weapon simultaneously moved backwards. He pointed the weapon to a blank wall and pulled a trigger. All the pins ejected at the same time and hit the wall in a straight line.

"Wow, that's awesome!" Axel exclaimed. He looked at the wall and saw that the pins automatically dropped, clearing the targeted space.

Ujin continued walking through the aisles and stopped at the next section. "These are 'zappers,' similar to the guns you have on earth. These use light energy instead of metal bullets." He looked at Axel who nodded. Then he picked up one of the zappers to show Axel its pistol grip and the small, glass monitor on top. He pointed it to one of the circular targets on the wall, and a laser beam was emitted when he pulled the trigger.

"As you can see, there are a variety of weapons here. It takes a lot of training to acquire the skill and mastery to use them."

"What kind of skills are you talking about? Do you think I can someday use them?

A female voice came from the door. "Huh, I doubt it."

Axel turned around and saw Isyna. She said, "I bet you can't handle even the tiniest weapon here."

Irritated by her remarks, Axel snapped back. "I may not have handled any, but I'm a quick study. I can be the best in using these weapons."

"Oh, really? Let's give that a try."

Isyna pulled out one of the small zappers, pointed it at the target on the wall, and pulled the trigger. The laser pierced through the target, and Isyna gave Axel a big grin. She handed him the weapon. "Now, your turn."

Shaking, Axel took the gun, aimed at the wall, and pulled the trigger. In his audacity, he rushed his aim, and the laser hit the ceiling lights instead of the target. Sparks exploded in the room like fireworks. He lost his balance and fell on the floor.

"Hmm, nice going. Quick study, huh!" She looked at him with an impish sneer. "Admit it, you can't handle it. I can't believe you're the chosen one. We're doomed."

"I just lost my balance—I can do it again."

He got up, regained his balance, and tried to aim the gun again. To his surprise, Ujin abruptly maneuvered to grab the weapon from Axel's hand.

Dismayed with Isyna's remarks, he said, "Isyna, I'll be training Axel on these weapons, but this is not the right time. He needs to return to his home now."

"Fine." Isyna turned around and left the room, and as she did so, she gave Axel an annoying stare and said, "I still do not believe he is the chosen one."

"Thank goodness, she's gone." Axel gave a sigh of relief. "What's with her? I do not think I did anything to offend her."

"Forget it. Just focus on what needs to be done. Right now, you must leave. The gateway allows passage for only a limited time, so let us not waste any more time."

"I do wanna go home, but I don't know how to get there."

"Here's a ring," Ujin said, gesturing for Axel to come closer. "Press the top and point it outward. Move your hand clockwise to form an imaginary oval shape in the air. That shape should create a vortex and transform into a portal leading to your world."

Axel followed what Ujin said and true enough, as he closed the oval figure, a wavy portal appeared. It was windy, and Axel felt like he was being pulled in.

"Bye, Axel. Be good."

Before Axel could answer, he was sucked into the vortex. He was so scared that he closed his eyes and let the force push him through. It felt like it would take forever, but an instant later, he popped out through the tapestry and landed with his face flat on the floor.

"Ouch" he cried. "I hate this!"

Suddenly, his bedroom door opened. His mom peeked in. "I heard a loud thump from your bedroom. Are you okay, Axel? Why are you on the floor?"

"Ah, I just had a bad dream."

"It's still night. Go back to sleep."

"'kay, mom."

He let out a sigh of relief, thankful that his mom did not see the tapestry, but then he remembered what Ujin said: no one but he can see the tapestry anyway.

The pain all over his body made it difficult for Axel to get up. He wanted to take a bath, but his exhaustion would not allow him to do so. He took off his shoes, changed into his pajamas, and laid in bed. He wished everything was just a bad dream, but as he closed his eyes to sleep, he felt the ring on his finger and realized that this was no longer a dream but his reality.

He had a destiny he needed to fulfill.

— CHAPTER 15 —

A Family Day

It was still winter break, and Axel was simply content to be home. He decided that the best use of his time was to write a journal about his new experience or rather weird adventure. *If people could read this, they'd think I'm crazy.* Although he was annoyed with events that he remembered, there were moments that made him smile and even laugh.

"What are you smiling about?" Leda asked, standing at the door. "What are you writing?"

Axel instantly closed his journal and said, "Nothing, just writing some notes."

"It's time for lunch. Come if you want to eat."

Axel kept his journal in his secret hiding place and went out to join everyone for lunch. It was Sunday, so Charles and Sarah didn't have to go to work.

Sarah started the conversation. "New semester is coming up. Do you need some things for school?"

Christa quickly responded, "I'd like new clothes."

"What? I just bought some for you before the school year started."

"But my older clothes are short and tight now. You know how fast I'm growing."

Sarah looked at Christa and realized how tall she'd really grown. "Fine, but not much."

Axel said, "I need a new backpack. The one I use has a hole, and the zipper is destroyed. I've been using it for two years."

Sarah nodded. "After we eat, we can head out to the store to buy the things you need. There might still be some sale items. Just remember we can't spend much. We'll just buy necessary things for school."

They were all quiet for the rest of the meal, and when they were finished, Sarah and Leda cleared the table while Christa and Axel changed their clothes. They headed for the stores in the city and spent their entire afternoon searching for and buying everything they needed.

When they returned to the car, Charles announced, "How would you like to have dinner in a restaurant?"

Sarah, who handled the family finances, stared at her husband with a displeased look. They had spent so much money at the store, and a restaurant dinner was doing to drain more of their funds. With Leda going college in a couple of months, money had become tight. Sarah was already thinking of how much more difficult it would be when Christa and Axel graduated high school.

"Yeah!" the kids excitedly answered in unison.

"It's settled. What kind of food do you want to eat?"

Remembering his meal with Queen Elyjanah, Axel was the first to respond. "I'd like burgers and fries."

"Me, too," said Christa.

"I'd like a steak dinner," Leda said.

Outnumbered by everyone, Sarah declared, "I know just the place to go. It's a fusion restaurant serving all sorts of dishes including steak dinner, burgers, and fries."

They happily loaded all the shopping bags in the trunk of the Oldsmobile and headed to the restaurant.

As they ate their choice dishes, they exchanged stories, plans, and even shared some jokes. Charles gave a toast to Leda on her acceptance to the college of her choice, to Christa for being the most valuable player and leading the basketball team to the championship, and to Axel to be promoted to the junior class in high school next semester. All in all, they had a wonderful, memorable family time.

Axel realized how much he loved his family and how much he cherished moments like these. Hiding his teary eyes, for now, he decided not to let them know of the destiny he had to fulfil in some faraway world. He promised himself that someday, he would.

— Chapter 16 —

Axel Returns to Zycodia

When Leda got to high school, Charles built an extension, so the girls each got their own rooms while Axel still occupied the smallest room in their house. He could have complained but the panoramic view of the city was worth staying in his smaller room. The best part was that his room had a special place to keep secrets.

When Axel was born, Charles converted this room from a storage to a nursery. He covered the exit door with a six-foot long piece of plywood and barricaded it with a cabinet. This was to prevent Axel from getting out of the house without their knowledge.

At the time Charles and Sarah bought their house, they did not yet have children. They used this room to store food, clothes, household supplies and even wood for the fireplace. Charles built compartments inside the closet to hide important documents and valuables.

One day, when Axel was clearing out his closet, he discovered these compartments. He was thrilled. Surely, this was the best place to hide his journals and any other item he did not want others to see. He saved some of his allowance to buy two locks, borrowed a screwdriver from his dad's toolbox, and added them to these compartments to make them secure. He even covered them with clothes. With two removable slabs on the wall, he was able to utilize this space to hide bigger items like the tapestry.

The day after their shopping trip, Axel organized all the new things he got. He transferred his books, pens, and notebooks into his new, bigger backpack. His new alarm clock was set next to his family picture. He put his new shirts and pants in the laundry for washing.

After organizing his new purchases, he decided to clean his room, including his secret hiding places. Upon opening those compartments, he saw the box containing the ring Ujin gave him, and memories of his journey to Zycodia flashed in his mind. This irritated him, and he threw the ring back inside.

That night, as he got ready for bed, his hand started to throb.

"Oh no, not again!" he exclaimed.

This was the sign he was dreading—the sign that meant he had to be transported to the other world—*again*. Remembering how he fell flat on the floor when he popped out of the tapestry, he decided to reposition his bed to face it, so when he came out, surely, he could land on the bed. Frustrated with his situation but satisfied with his strategy, he then took the ring and placed it on his finger.

The tapestry started waving and then transforming into an unstable portal. Axel grabbed his shoes but before he could put them on, he was pulled into the tunnel.

He yelled as he rapidly traversed through this space. In an instant, he was pushed out and dropped on the floor. Disoriented he cried, "Now where am I?"

Before he stood up, he put his shoes on and straightened himself up. He was surprised to see Ujin and Queen Elyjanah who, this time, was not wearing casual clothes but a long, purple gown with a golden sash on her waist. She was truly beautiful.

"Hello, Axel. I trust your travel was not as difficult as the last time," she said.

Ujin was as stiff as he was before. This time, he was wearing some sort of protective armor on his chest and arms, making him look more rigid.

"It was still hard. It felt like my body was being pulled apart."

"It will get easier with each transport. I know it," Ujin assured him.

The queen gestured toward the couch. "Please sit. You have been summoned here to commence your journey, your destiny."

"Are you sure I'm the chosen one?" Axel pleaded. "Why not you or Ujin or any of your warriors? How about Isyna? She doesn't think I'm the one."

"That is true, Axel. We are not certain that you are the chosen one. I cannot, in good conscience, let you face all the dangers of this mission without knowing that it is truly your destiny to help save our kingdom. While you have the sign, there must not be any doubt."

"How do we do that?"

She pointed, "Behind that door is our sacred celestial room, our sanctuary. It was built by our ancestors long ago. In there, you must face an important test. Should you survive it, you will have no choice but to fulfill your destiny. If you fail, you will be returned to earth, and all knowledge of our world will be erased from your memory. If you do pass this test and choose not fulfill your destiny, your life will be haunted by nightmares."

"You said that I will be haunted in my dreams. Will there be any cure?" Axel asked. "It seems like my life will be one big mess. That's so unfair."

"Before you worry about what may not come to pass, do this test first, so we can figure out how to face the future. How about it, Axel?" the queen asked.

"Will this test hurt?"

"I do not know because I have never had to take that test," Ujin answered. "Are you ready?"

"I guess I have no choice," Axel replied with a sigh.

With that, the queen signaled to Ujin and said, "Let's begin."

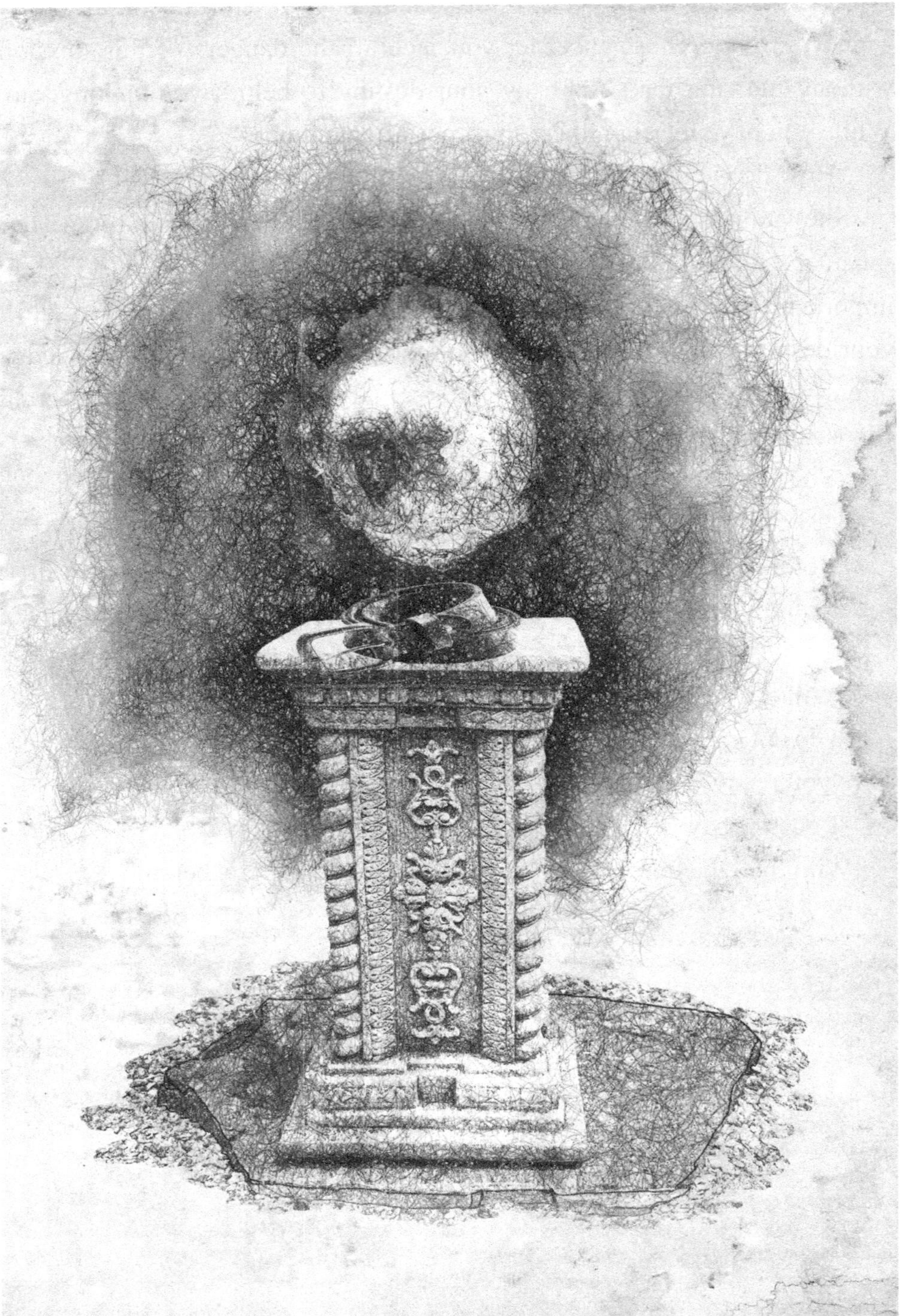

— Chapter 17 —

The Test

Ujin inserted the key to the lock while Queen Elyjanah placed her hand on a glass panel above the lock. The door opened, and she went inside followed by Axel. Ujin stayed behind to guard the door.

A nostalgic feeling overwhelmed Axel, as he entered the sacred room. It was a circular chamber enclosed with twelve vertical wall panels and a domed ceiling. Each panel had images similar to those on his tapestry.

As Queen Elyjanah pressed a button on a remote control, the ceiling slowly lifted upward, exposing the gentle sunlight streaming through beautiful panels of stained glass.

Providing illumination at the center of the room was an orb that rested on a pedestal which was on top of three steps—the sight was mesmerizing. There was a golden belt wrapped with the ends clasped together underneath the orb. Axel looked closer and saw the symbols etched around it, again, twelve of them.

"Go closer to the center."

Axel nodded then hesitantly inched forward to the pedestal.

"That's a good first sign. If the orb does not shine, then it's time for you to go home. This is a good sign, as the orb is still shining. You need to place your right hand on top of the orb. Make sure the entire surface of your palm is pressed on it. A surge of energy will run through your body for several minutes. If you are the chosen one, you will be able to take possession of the belt. If the belt does not come to you, that means this destiny is not yours, and you will be transported back to your home."

"If I fail and am returned home, I will not remember you and everything about this world, right?"

"It is for your own good."

"Take a deep breath, relax, step forward, and follow my instructions. I believe in you." She gave Axel a comforting smile then left the room.

Following the queen's instructions, he took a deep breath and climbed the steps to get closer to the pedestal. He hesitated, wondering if it was worth it. He was so scared that his heartrate went up. When he was close enough to the pedestal, he rested his shaking hand on the orb.

The instant his palm touched the orb, the glow intensified and enveloped the tip of his fingers. It felt like a jolt of electricity shooting up through his fingers, and the pain grew as it enclosed his hand. He wanted to end the connection but was not able to. It was like his hand was glued to the orb. The glow crept up his arm higher and higher toward his head. When it reached the top of his head, the glow slowly descended to his feet. As his body absorbed the energy, he was lifted two feet from the ground.

For three long minutes, Axel endured extreme pain until it ebbed, enabling him to open his eyes. The belt that was around the orb unwound from the pedestal and floated toward Axel. It circled his body as if it had a mind of its own then wrapped around his waist. The glowing energy receded into the orb, and Axel dropped to the ground with a crashing sound.

The queen opened the door and found Axel unconscious. She signaled to Ujin, who carried Axel out of the room and placed him on the queen's couch. For several hours, he sank into a deep, deep sleep.

When he awoke, he saw the queen, Ujin and even Isyna staring at him. He tried to sit up, but a splitting headache made him fall back on the couch.

"Lay still, Axel," the queen ordered. He stayed down and tried not to move an inch. Remembering what just happened, he felt his waist to see if the belt was actually on him, and it was.

Queen Elyjanah said, "Yes, the belt is now yours. It is official: our world, our survival now rests in your hands."

Isyna sneered. "So, you're really the one… unbelievable!"

The queen placed her hand on Axel's forehead. He felt as if the queen was extracting the pain, and it made him feel better. Still feeling weak from the experience, he stayed on the couch a little longer. He raised his head to look at the belt and then let his fingers run along the symbols around it.

"How am I supposed to save your kingdom? I am just a kid. I don't have any power or even special skills."

"Don't get ahead of yourself. You have a brilliant mind. Just take it one step at a time." The queen sat beside him. "We are concerned that another celestial gem was stolen, so it is crucial that your mission begins immediately. The final goal is to retrieve all twelve gems and merge them with the belt. You will be the focal point of this operation. Once the belt is whole, it will be the strongest weapon we can harness to defeat our enemies and save our world. Do not be afraid, and believe in yourself, as I have faith in you. Ujin and I, with many trusted Zycodians, will guide you along the way." She glanced at Isyna. "My daughter will also be able to help you, right Isyna?"

"Yeah, fine," she said reluctantly.

Axel suddenly remembered that school was to start the following Monday. "Can I go home now? My school starts on Monday. My family would be wondering where I'd be if I can't go home."

The queen said, "Yes, Axel, you may go, but before you do so, go back to the sacred chamber and return the belt."

He did as he was told. When he unfastened the belt, he was surprised to see that it floated back to its resting place on its own. He looked around at the room again and wondered how passing the test would alter the course of his life.

"Good-bye for now. We will anxiously wait for your return."

The queen and Ujin waved to Axel.

Isaya pouted and crossed her arms then muttered a quiet goodbye.

Axel pointed the ring above his head and moved his hand to create the portal which rapidly pulled him through the tunnel. At least, this time, he was consoled by the thought of landing on his bed. He popped out of the tapestry and landed on the floor with a thump... again.

His mom opened the door. "Goodness. Why are you on the floor again? I saw your bed was out of place, so I moved it back to where it should be."

"Please leave my bed alone next time."

"Okay," she said with a wondering look.

When she left the room, Axel took off the ring and returned it to his hiding place. He was too exhausted to think about what happened further, so he slumped on his bed and fell asleep.

— CHAPTER 18 —

Axel's Mission Begins

Axel settled into his junior year at school. To avoid worrying about the challenges being forced on him in the other world, he decided to bury himself in his studies.

The beginning of the year saw him at the top of his class excelling in all his subjects. He submitted assignments diligently, getting perfect scores on quizzes and tests. He joined clubs and took on additional responsibilities as class treasurer and president of the math and science clubs. For two weeks, he enjoyed his life as a simple student, making new friends and keeping company with his old ones. He even found time to help other classmates struggling with their lessons.

One Friday, while he was in the middle of a morning math class, his right hand started to throb. The pain was tolerable enough to bear until school was over in the afternoon. With his backpack dangling loosely from his shoulder and ignoring good-byes from his friends, he hurriedly walked home. As the pain increased, he had no choice but to run faster and faster. As soon as he closed the front door, his hand started glowing. Thankful that no one was home yet, he rushed to his bedroom, dropped his backpack on the floor, and locked his door.

Already familiar with the drill, he took his ring and placed his hand on the tapestry. In an instant, he was whirled into the tunnel and plopped out in the other world. This time, he landed on a bush.

"Ouch," he cried again. "I really, really, really hate these landings."

Trying to untangle his body from the branches was a real pain until he felt them being pulled away. This allowed him to wiggle out and free himself from the bush. He turned to find out who helped him. No one was in sight except for a goat munching on some grass. The goat was white from head to short tail. Its fur was straight, and its head was accentuated by brown horns that arched backwards. All in all, Axel thought it was a unique, good-looking animal.

Axel stared at the goat.

The goat stared back at him.

Axel laughed a bit and said, "Why not? In this world, anything's possible." He looked into the goat's eyes. "Did you just help me get out of the bush?"

The goat did not answer.

"Oh, what the heck! And I thought everything here was magical. Guess you're not." He got up and started to move away from the goat. Suddenly, the goat poked his behind with its horns.

"Ouch," Axel cried. "What in the world did you do that for?"

The goat still did not answer.

Axel turned away but the goat poked him again.

"Stop it. Now I think you can understand me." Axel looked around and saw a loose branch. He picked it up, held it like a sword, and pointed it at the animal. "You wanna fight, you silly, old goat?"

Without warning, it jumped on him. Axel fell backwards, pinned to the ground by the goat on his chest.

"I'm a silly old goat, huh?" it angrily yelled. "I helped free you from the bush and didn't get even a 'thank you' from you. You even dare to fight with me! You can't even defend yourself, stupid, wimpy kid."

Still on the ground, Axel tried to grab the goat's horns with both his hands to free himself. They struggled and rolled back and forth until Ujin appeared and separated them.

"Enough of this fight. There are real dangers out there, and you two decided to fight each other!" Ujin scolded them both. "Axel, this is Rolin. He is from the Capricorn tribe."

Rolin straightened his four legs and slowly raised his body. He stood up on his hind legs and transformed into a human figure. He was shorter than Ujin and had grayish hair, beady eyes, and a goatee that made him look much older than Ujin.

Shaking his head, he said, "Ujin, I know I owe you for saving my life."

Ujin nodded sternly. "Glad to know you remembered. Do you also recall your promise?"

"Yes, I promised that whenever there is a need, I will always be there to help, but you never mentioned I was to babysit a child!" With a subdued look, he signed. "Nevertheless, I shall do as you ask."

He reached out his hand to help Axel stand up. "I go now. Remember, I will be keeping a close eye on you." Rolin transformed back into a goat, walked away, and disappeared through the thick bushes.

"Looks like you are ready to go. The Cancer tribe's celestial gem is the first you need to get." His Swifty appeared with just the wave of his hand.

"Why that tribe, and what kind of beings are they?"

The roof door opened, and Ujin signaled Axel to get it. "You've already met a member of that tribe—remember Riqui? Their tribe is the first because they may be in danger of being invaded, and you need to get their gem."

"Why not the gem that was stolen?

"That mission is more complicated. Plus, you need to collect two other gems and undergo training first, but it is time to go." The jet lifted off and zoomed ahead at super speed.

— CHAPTER 19 —

Riqui, the Cancer Warrior

At high velocity, Axel did not even see where they were going, until the jet stopped. Axel and Ujin jumped out, and, to Axel's surprise, the jet settled into Ujin's parking space by itself. Axel wondered, *could this moving machine have a mind of its own?* He shook his head, thinking how foolish that would be if that was the case, but then again, based on the other things he'd seen in this world, it could be true.

"I thought we were going to the tribe of the Cancers. Why are we back here?"

Ujin did not answer. Instead, he dragged Axel to the elevator shaft that whirled them to the highest level, queen's chambers. When the capsule opened, he saw Queen Elyjanah and Isyna waiting. The queen greeted him with a smile.

"Hello again, Axel. How are you doing?"

"I'm fine."

"Before you head out to your first challenge, you put on the belt. It is of utmost importance that you wear it most of the time while you are here. It is also for your protection. In moments of imminent danger, touch the gem at the center of your belt. It will alert me of your situation."

Queen Elyjanah accompanied Axel to the celestial gem room. He climbed the first step and then touched the belt. It unwound, descended, and wrapped itself around his waist. The queen handed Axel a sash. "This is to cover your belt. It is lightweight and makes your belt invisible. You cannot allow others to see that you are wearing it. Only the tribal chief and his most trusted warrior know of your arrival, so we must make sure your identity is protected. Most important of all, we cannot allow our enemies to know about you. Should they get wind of your presence and your purpose, you will truly be in grave danger."

Axel tied the sash over the belt. For more security, he tucked in his shirt under his pants.

"Ujin, please give him a communicator."

Ujin handed it to Axel. "Wear it on your wrist just like a watch."

"What is this for?"

"Only leaders of each clan have learned how to speak your language. For those who have not been trained, the communicator acts as a translator. When the individual talks, you will hear it in your language and vice versa; your listener will understand you in their own dialect. Ujin will take you where you need to go. For every gem that you need to collect, you will first have to prove yourself worthy for it to be given to you." The queen paused for a moment, and her features softened. "I am truly sorry that this burden was placed upon you. We will do everything in our power to aid and protect you in this quest, but these challenges are for you and you alone to face. Your greatest weapon is your mind. Always remember that. I wish you luck, Axel, and be safe."

"Thank you, your majesty," he said, bowing.

Ujin and Axel went down the elevator shaft to the fifth level, where the twelve doors were located. Ujin led Axel to the door that had the symbol that was also on his tapestry. As they entered the room, Axel was surprised by how large it was. There was a couch, some chairs, and a table in the middle of the room. Artifacts, statuettes, and figurines of tiny crabs were inside a glass cabinet on one of the walls, and a large painting of an island was hanging on another side of the room. There was a fountain in another corner. What was odd was that the fountain looked more like a pond. Water flowed from the wall. There was another door located across from the entrance. He was about to ask where that door led when Ujin signaled for him to follow.

They circled past the table and exited through the other door to face what looked like an endless tunnel. Ujin summoned his jet with the wave of his hand. Its roof opened, and they both stepped inside. The seat belt was still wrapping around him when the vehicle powered up and sped through the dark tunnel. In a few minutes, a bright light appeared, as they reached the end of the tunnel, and from an invisible portal, they landed on the seashore. Ujin pressed one of the buttons on the dashboard, the engine turned off, and they hopped out onto the ground.

Axel had to adjust his eyes to the brightness and took a deep breath to settle his nerves. Seeing the clear, blue sky that stretched for miles, he remembered the first time he set foot on this world, the green sand, red sky, and red ocean. Surprisingly, the rippling sounds of the water helped calm him down. Across from where they stood, he caught sight of a huge island. The panoramic, breathtaking view of the sky and the ocean that circled around the island seemed to put him in a trance. A giant crab emerged from the water and jumped in front of Axel, shattering his peaceful moment.

"You again!" Axel yelled.

"Aren't you happy to see me?" the crab said, transforming into his human form. "Riqui, at your service." His hand shifted back into a claw, and he made a salute gesture.

To Axel, Riqui was a mean-looking crab, but as a person, he had a gentle face with strong features. His curved lips made him appear to be always smiling, which softened the intensity of his piercing black eyes. Axel guessed that Riqui was taller than him by a foot. Thick, messy, dark red hair gave him additional height. The tight shirt and pants he wore reminded Axel of scuba divers back on earth.

Ujin cleared his throat. "Axel, Riqui hails from the tribe of Cancers. Their community is based on that island." He gestured toward the group of islands ahead. "They are fearless but fun-loving people. Your first task is to retrieve their celestial gem."

"How can I go there? I don't even know how to swim."

"What? You can't swim?" Riqui grinned. "The water is shallow, so why don't you just try to walk through it?"

"Fine." Despite his bravado, as Axel grew closer to the water's edge, his earlier unease returned. He peered over his shoulder to see Ujin and Riqui smiling and waving at him. With a huff, Axel stomped into the water. Seeing that the water was actually shallow, Axel's confidence grew, and he ambled toward the group of islands. However, after the initial ten feet, the water level rose, and before he knew it, the water was up to his chin. He spun around and cried out, "This is too deep for me. I can't go—"

"You are such a wimp! Wimpy, wimpy, wimpy!" Riqui chanted.

Axel returned to shore, and as he stepped on the sand, he splashed some water on Riqui.

"Stop it!" Ujin exclaimed. "Riqui, you know how important this mission is. Stop taunting him."

"Axel, I cannot accompany you on your journey. Riqui will be the one to give assistance to you. I shall come back to fetch you here when you are done."

Riqui bent down. "Come on, then. Hop on my back."

"What?" Axel questioned.

"Are you just gonna stand there? Hop on."

Axel thought it was crazy, but he clung to Riqui's back, and as he proceeded to the water, lo and behold, Riqui transformed into a giant crab.

Axel wasn't sure how to adjust his grip. Afraid to drown, he just hung on tightly as they crossed the water. On the way, Riqui intentionally dunked below water level, making his passenger drop down, too. Axel panicked when he went underwater and tried to raise his body. As he did so, mischievous Riqui floated upward, making Axel lose his balance.

Riqui played this trick on Axel twice, but after the third time, Axel smacked him between the eyes and yelled, "Stop doing that!" Riqui was laughing and having a good time, but because he was in crab form, Axel couldn't tell what was going on.

Upon reaching the island, Riqui shifted back into his human form.

"Now, what should I do?" Axel asked.

"Well, first, you need to meet our chief elder, that way," he said, pointing.

The island was surrounded by trees. He saw other people and crabs everywhere. Some were just walking. Some were in groups chatting. There was even a pair of crabs that were fighting.

Axel followed his guide toward a swamp area where the water seemed shallow. Houses mostly made of shells were clustered in this area. At the front entrance, there were several huge shell-like structures laying on the water. The were of varying sizes and tied to trees. Axel assumed they functioned like boats. Riqui untied the rope of one from the tree and signaled Axel to get in, which he did with a hop.

"Why did you have to hop?"

"Don't know, seeing these shell boats, I just felt like doing it. Kinda making sure they are sturdy, safe enough.

Riqui sneered and picked up the oar clamped to the edge of the shell. As he rowed through passageways, a new thought occurred to Axel.

"Riqui, if people here can swim like crabs, why do they need these boat things?"

"Use your brain. Don't you think they can have friends, visitors, business people who come here, who are not of the Cancer tribe and can't swim... just like you?"

"Oh, I did not realize that."

Axel had never seen a place like this. He looked around, trying to absorb every detail of the scenery. The houses resting partly under water were not made of wood. Of course, Axel realized wood was not the best thing to use for a house on water. Some windows looked like they were made of clear glass. There were coral reefs in front of some houses with weeds for decorations.

Some of the houses were domed, covered in shells, and didn't seem to have any openings. "Riqui, how do people go inside those homes?"

"They mostly enter from the water under the house."

Riqui saw Axel's questioning look and sighed. "We need to be near water constantly. That's why we have our houses on water. We use rocks, shells, and other special materials from under the sea to build them." Riqui pointed to one of the biggest houses in the inner section of the community. "There, that's where we are going."

Axel remained silent as Riqui steered the boat closer to their destination.

— CHAPTER 20 —

The Cancer Challenge

Upon arrival, Riqui tied the shell boat securely to one of the poles in front of the house. There were two other rafts parked in what Axel likened to driveways on earth.

Riqui stepped onto the deck that extended three feet from the front wall of the house. Axel followed. Together, they walked towards the door. Before Riqui could knock, a voice from inside called out. "Get in here."

The door opened by itself.

Riqui went in. Axel followed.

There was an old man sitting with legs crossed on a stone chair. He was almost bald. His beady eyes were closed, so Axel thought he was asleep. He wore a red vest with a necklace made of shells. A blanket skirt covered the rest of his body. He was stiff but sat in a regal posture. There was no doubt he was the chief elder. Riqui bowed to the old man and forced Axel's head down into bow as well.

"Good sire."

"Ah, Riqui, I thought that was you. Your smell betrays you." He smiled, but Riqui seemed annoyed and tried to smell himself.

"I brought Axel here to meet you."

"Come closer, my eyes are not that good."

Axel moved forward. The chief's hand shifted into a claw and thwacked Axel's head.

"Ouch, what did you do that for?"

"Heh, heh, heh, you have a thick head… good, good. Do you know who I am?"

"You are the chief elder."

"You got that right… smart, smart too." The chief grinned. "I'm Boscoe.

I've been the chief here for ages. Riqui is my right hand, or you can say my right claw, my most trusted... heh, heh, heh... crab. So, you are here to get our celestial gem."

"That's what I was told to do."

"Not that easy. You must first prove you are worthy of having it."

"How am I supposed to do that?"

"Hmm... young and impatient, are you?" With a sigh, he said, "Very well. Under my house, there is a chest about this big." He motioned with his hands to show the length and width. "If you really are the one, it will appear to you. If you are not, there is no way will you see it. So, go that way." He pointed to the back of his house. Riqui walked with Axel in that direction. There was no floor in that section; instead, it was an opening to the water underneath.

Riqui said, "This is where you have to dive down and look for a chest."

"I told you I can't swim!" Axel protested.

"You really are such a wimp."

"That's not true. I just never learned how."

"Yeah, yeah. This time the water is not that deep. Just bring down your head and look for it. Take a deep breath before you go down."

"Fine." Axel took a deep breath and then submerged himself in the water.

Riqui watched and started laughing, as he sat down.

After a minute or two, Axel emerged and grabbed the top of the opening.

Riqui couldn't contain himself and burst out laughing.

Axel frowned, annoyed. "What are you laughing about?"

"Did you find the chest?" Riqui asked.

"No," he answered with a frown.

"Of course, not. You'll never find the chest that way. Try opening your eyes, silly."

Axel splashed some water on him and went down again. This time, he opened his eyes. Adjusting to the water environment was hard, but he tried to focus. He looked straight ahead and turned clockwise to search for the chest. He saw nothing and, being almost out of breath, emerged from the water again.

"So, nothing?" asked Riqui.

"What do you think?" He shook the water out of his face. "Do you see anything in my hands? This is crazy. Why should I be doing this? I'm perfectly happy just going to school and being with my family and friends."

"Now, now. Don't despair. Try again."

Axel hesitated, then slowly sank down again.

He focused his eyes to look farther this time and slowly turned around. He noticed a school of little fish swimming in one direction. He followed the fish and saw something shiny halfway buried in the ground. He moved toward the object and realized it was a treasure chest with some jewels that glittered on top.

Axel was almost out of breath, but he moved toward it. He grabbed the chest and, with all his strength, yanked it out of the ground. He burst out of the water and placed the chest on the floor on top of the water. He tried to climb out of the opening, but his waterlogged clothes were dragging him down.

Riqui helped Axel out of the water and grinned. "See? I knew you could do it. Take the chest, and let's go back to the chief."

They both walked back to the front, where the chief was sitting.

"Sire," Riqui called.

Maybe, this time, he really was asleep.

"Sire" Riqui called again, louder, shaking his hand.

"What?" The chief sat up. "What's going on?"

"Axel is back with the chest."

"What chest?" Boscoe blinked, still in a fog.

"…the chest that you wanted him to find," Riqui replied with a sigh.

"…him…who?"

"Axel, remember? We got here a few hours ago. His goal is to retrieve our celestial gem, but he first needs to prove his worth. For starters, you wanted him to look for the chest."

"My eyes are not that sharp anymore, so come here and let me look at you again."

Axel came closer, and the chief thwacked Axel's head with his claw.

"Ouch!" Axel cried.

"Oh yeah, now I remember your head. So, where's the chest?"

Axel placed it in front of the chief.

"Open it and bring out what's inside," the chief ordered.

Axel obeyed. Inside, there was a scroll that had some sort of writing etched on it. The chief slowly reached for it.

"Sit next to me."

Axel sat down, wondering why the chest was dry inside. Afraid of being hit again, he kept his questions to himself.

"Come on, tell me what you see." The chief insisted.

Staring curiously at the scroll, he replied, "Some sort of writings, but I don't know what they mean."

"That's because the writings are in our language. Through the years, Ujin has been teaching us your language. Here's what the writing says."

The chief waved his hand over the scroll. It started to glow, and the words suddenly appeared legible to Axel, who was too amazed to even speak.

Suddenly, he felt a thwack on this head that startled him. Looking at the words, Axel read them aloud:

> *Upon a coral reef,*
> *lay weeds in keep,*
> *A pearl to hide,*
> *the hope inside.*

"What's that supposed to mean?" Axel asked.

The chief snorted. "Huh? That's your problem. Figure out what it means, and when you do," Boscoe paused to snort again, "you'll be able to find the gem you are looking for. Now, remember the words, then put back the scroll inside the chest. When you are done, return it where you got it from in the water and get out of here so I can go back to my nap."

"What if someone else were to look for the treasure? Would they see the same words?

The chief shook his head. "These words are for you only."

Axel read the words again then put the shell back in the chest. When he dove back into the water, he found the hole from which he'd pulled the chest. To his surprise, as soon as he placed the chest back in the hole, it disappeared.

Riqui and Axel left the chief, who was already asleep. They went out of the house and stepped onto the boat again. Riqui paddled back to the entrance of the community and tied the boat back to its original place. Axel felt the warm sand on the seashore when they disembarked.

Axel noticed his ring starting to light up. "Riqui," Axel called pointing to his ring. "I can't stay any longer. I must go home."

"Well then, we don't have a choice, do we? Alright, hop on my back, and we'll swim back to the mainland." This time, Riqui swam faster than he had before. Upon reaching the shore, he yelled, "Bye, Axel. Until next time."

Ujin arrived to fetch Axel. Hurriedly, he waved for his jet, and they rode back to the castle as fast as the jet could take them.

Queen Elyjanah smiled. "Axel, how was your journey?"

"It was okay, but I did not find the celestial gem yet. Only thing I got was a poem. I have to decipher its meaning."

"Well, that's a start. Please return the belt to the sacred room."

Axel did so and gave the sash back to the queen.

"That, you can keep, but make sure to always bring it with you when you come here."

Axel pointed the ring above his head and formed the imaginary oval shape. The portal opened and pulled Axel into the tunnel. Axel remembered how he dropped from the tapestry. He realized that he forgot to set his bed to the place where he knew he'd land. He dreaded the pain, and surely enough, he tumbled out of the tapestry and onto the floor. It was too painful to move, so he ended up sleeping on the floor.

— CHAPTER 21 —

Back Home

Axel woke up to the growling of his stomach. He slowly sat up and tried to remember everything that had happened to him. His clothes dried up with the sash still wrapped around his waist, but there was no belt. He took off the sash and ring and hid them in his secret storage.

"Axel," he heard his mom call. "Time to eat supper."

As hungry as he was, he waddled out of his room and made a beeline for his seat. Christa and Leda followed behind. Leda sat next to Axel. She seemed to smell something weird in the dining room. She sniffed at everything and realized that the smell came from Axel.

"Phew, Axel, why do you smell like... like... geez, I don't know. What is that smell?"

Christa stood up and went around the table to smell Axel.

"Go away!" exclaimed Axel.

Christa said, "You smell like crab!"

Embarrassed and upset, he stomped out of the dining area and went straight to the bathroom to take a bath. He knew his sisters would never stop taunting him about the crab smell. Even if he was hungry, he did enjoy the bath. When he was done, he felt and smelled heavenly clean.

The beef stew Sarah cooked smelled so good. However, when he returned to the dinner table, his bowl was empty. "No more food left?"

"Hold on. I left some for you." Sarah stood up and filled his bowl.

Axel was so hungry that he finished the rest of the food in just a few minutes. With his recent water encounters, he was glad his mom hadn't cooked any seafood.

Being the last to finish eating, he had to do the dishes. He did not mind doing it this time. He was just glad to be home again.

Back in his room, he opened his backpack to look at his planner. All he saw was a whole list of homework. He gathered the books, pens, and notepads. He needed to solve problems for algebra, read two chapters for history, and write an essay for English.

He decided to tackle the required reading for history, but after going through three pages, Axel realized that he did not understand what he was reading. His thoughts kept going back to the other world. Frustrated that he was not able to concentrate on his studies, he pulled out his journal to write his latest experiences while they were still fresh in his mind.

When he got to the part with the riddle on the scroll inside the treasure chest, he had a hard time recalling the words. He recited it twenty times over until he finally got them right. He immediately wrote them down… *Upon a coral reef, lay weeds in keep; a pearl to hide the hope inside.* He thought of all possible answers to the riddle, but nothing came to mind.

Frustrated that he had more questions than answers, he put his journal back in his secret place and then went to bed. His mind kept repeating the riddle until he fell asleep.

— Chapter 22 —

Rena

Over the next few weeks, Axel hardly had time to dwell on the mysterious riddle, as his schoolwork picked up. Soon, all his teachers were assigning semester-long projects that were due at the end of the year. Even though his peers groaned at the workload, Axel was grateful for the distraction. He even tried to join the band by pleading with the music director, who was concerned about Axel's workload. The director caved but added the stipulation that if his other grades started to fall, Axel would be kicked out.

Outside of classes, despite a very busy schedule, he fulfilled his duties as the class treasurer and president of the math and science clubs. He also found time to play basketball with his friends after school even if he was not that athletic. All he wanted was to have fun, but try as he might, thoughts of the other world kept flashing in his mind.

In his math and science classes, there was a girl who caught his eye. Her name was Rena Davis. She was pretty and smart. Her grades were comparable to Axel's. As the days went by, he found himself getting more and more interested in her. He wanted to talk to her and be with her all the time. The problem was that his shyness always got in the way. Dennis kept on pushing him to do so and took every opportunity to get them together.

That chance did come for Axel. He was taking Advanced Placement class for science and his science teacher scheduled a special project for everyone in class, and by luck, he was paired with Rena. As excited as he was, he tried not to show his true emotions. They were given a few minutes before the class period ended to plan for the project. When they sat together, his heart rate picked up.

Rena broke the silence. "Do you have any idea how we can tackle this project?"

Axel hesitated. "Hmm… hmm… not yet. We can… hmm… maybe we can first start listing whatever idea comes to mind."

"Sounds good," answered Rena. "The class is almost over. How about if we meet after class to discuss our plan?"

"Great. Let's meet at the cafeteria around 3:15."

"Sure, I'll see you then."

The bell rang. The students dispersed to go to other classes. Axel proceeded to the band room for practice. Elated, he played the trombone so much better than usual that his teacher complimented him.

Axel reached the lunch area promptly at 3:15. Rena was not there yet. Hoping that she did not forget their meeting, he settled his backpack down and sat on the bench, unaware that he was fidgeting so much. Only five minutes passed by, but for Axel, it seemed like forever.

"Sorry I'm a bit late. I had to get some papers from Mr. Jones." Rena's voice came from behind him.

Surprised, Axel instantly jumped to his feet, bumping the table in front of him.

Rena tried her best not to laugh and spoke apologetically. "Oh, I didn't mean to startle you, I'm sorry."

"That's okay," Axel replied, as he straightened his legs.

"We can start our list now, but I can't stay long. I have to be home by 3:40 to babysit my little brother. My dad has to go to work, and my mom comes home from work at around 5:30. How would you like to walk home with me, and we can continue working at my house?"

"Sure, if you don't mind. Do you live close by?"

"Yeah, just a block away."

On the way to Rena's house, they talked about anything and everything that came to mind. They were enjoying the conversation when Rena announced, "We're here."

Only then did Axel realize that her place was not far from his home. Rena unlocked the door with her key and let him in. Andrew, Rena's dad, stepped into the living room dressed and ready to leave for work. She introduced Axel to her dad and told him that they had a project to work on.

"Have to run. Your brother is taking a nap, and mom will be home soon. Nice to meet you, Axel."

The afternoon went by fast in Axel's mind. They finished discussing their plan in two hours, and by the time they were done, Rena's mom arrived home.

"Mom, this is Axel. We just finished discussing our science project."

"Hi, nice to meet you, Axel. What's your science project about?"

"We're supposed to do an experiment called "Drop test". We need to gather items to drop from maybe the roof to check the time and velocity of each drop.

"That's very interesting." Rena's mom saw Axel collecting his books and added, "Are you getting ready to go, Axel?"

"Yes, and I think we came up with a pretty good plan for the project," he answered. Turning to Rena, he said, "Thanks for the time. I'll see you tomorrow."

"Bye," she nodded and led him out. As she closed the door, she saw her mom smiling. "What's funny?"

Her mom chuckled as she went to the bedroom without answering her.

Meanwhile, Axel walked home happily, unaware that he was skipping every now and then. From the time their project was assigned, not once had he thought of the "other world."

— CHAPTER 23 —

The Search Begins

School days went by. Axel and Rena submitted their project and got a glowing "A" for a grade on it. The best thing that came out of the project was the friendship that started to grow between them. They studied together and even formed a study group to help some classmates with their lessons.

Zycodia was now far from Axel's mind, until one afternoon during class. At first, he felt only a dull throbbing in his right hand and tried to ignore it. The pain increased by the minute, and when it became unbearable, he asked permission to go to the nurse's office. He claimed to have a splitting headache and was allowed to go home.

Not again, he thought on his way home. He was so upset that as soon as he entered his bedroom, he threw his backpack on the bed... *why me? I really hate this.*

Because he did not know how long he had to stay in the other world, he took a bath and then packed some snacks. He put on the ring and tied the sash around his waist. With a huge sigh, he placed his hand on the tapestry and was transported back to Zycodia. He landed in the castle where the queen was waiting for him. Without further instructions, he went inside the sanctuary room, touched the belt and it wrapped around his waist. He then covered it with the sash. "Good luck, Axel," said the queen smiling.

Ujin led Axel back to the fifth floor where they exited to get to Ujin's jet. They were immediately hurled to the Cancer district where they landed near the shore. There, he saw Riqui waiting for them.

Hands on his waist, towering over Axel, Riqui said, "Hey, hey, hey... did you miss me?"

"Not really." He stood up and fixed his shirt.

"So, have you figured out the answer to the riddle?"

"No, I didn't even wanna remember it."

"Then what are you doing here? Go home."

"I can't. The pain in my hand won't stop."

"Well, then you have no choice, do you?" Riqui exclaimed as he sat on a rock that was lying close by. "Do you remember the words?"

"Yeah, it goes 'Upon a coral reef, lay weeds in keep; a pearl to hide the hope inside.' Do you know what it means?"

"Nope, and it's your job to find out the answer."

"Fine. My first thought is just to consider the literal meaning of the words, so there should be a place here where there are weeds and coral reefs, right? Is there a place in this island where we can find those things?"

"Huh... Of course, there are lots of those in this island. Where do you want to look?"

"Geez. I don't know. Anywhere? Everywhere? Besides, you're the one who lives here, you should know," Axel retorted.

They both fell silent for a few minutes thinking.

"Oh, oh...! I have an idea... can you climb a tree?" Axel asked.

"Yeah, but climbing is not my thing. I don't like high places. I do have a friend who is a very good climber. We can go to him and ask his help."

"Let's go," Axel said.

Riqui stood up, and they both started to go through the trees. They rode on one of the shell boats again, and Riqui paddled through the houses. While doing so, he said to Axel, "Can we really not tell anyone the reason why you are here?"

Axel nodded.

"I will introduce you as a friend from the inland. Oh, and cover your sash."

Axel untucked his shirt and tucked the sash into his pants. "Is this better?"

"Sure," Riqui said.

They passed the chief's house, but they continued until they reached

Riqui's friend's house on the farthest side of the island. Riqui parked the boat, walked to the front, and knocked on the door. "Hojo, it's Riqui!"

The door opened. A man stepped out pointing a knife at Riqui, who fell backwards. Axel saved him from falling into the water.

"What do you want?"

"Is that the way to greet a friend?" Riqui asked as he landed a punch on Hojo, launching him back into the house.

Axel followed Riqui into the house but at a safe distance. To his surprise, when Hojo got up, he and Riqui gave each other a big hug.

"Fooled you, didn't we?" Riqui said to Axel. "This is Hojo."

"Hojo, this is my friend Axel from the mainland. He is doing a research project on our island. He is in search of seashells, weeds, and coral reefs. His idea is to climb a tree and have an aerial view to find where they are. You, my friend, are the best crab climber."

"That I am. That I am." Hojo said, nodding in agreement. "I'll help you out, but first, we eat. Have a seat."

Hojo came back with a bowl of seaweed. "Join me."

Riqui grabbed some.

Not wanting to insult hospitality, Axel said, "No thank you, I just ate."

With Hojo and Riqui eating, not a single strand of seaweed was left in the bowl. "That was good," Hojo commented as he rubbed his tummy.

"Sure was. I feel like going to sleep now," Riqui replied.

Axel felt a bit disgusted with the way they ate and what they ate. He thought, seaweed... yuck.

After Hojo cleared the table, he said, "Now let's go climb a tree. By the way, what kind of seashells or weeds are you looking for?"

"Not sure. Why, are there several kinds of weeds?"

"Of course, there are different kinds of weeds. Some are short, some are long, some are thin, and some are thick."

Riqui started laughing.

"Gee, I don't know. Maybe Riqui knows. He thinks this is so funny."

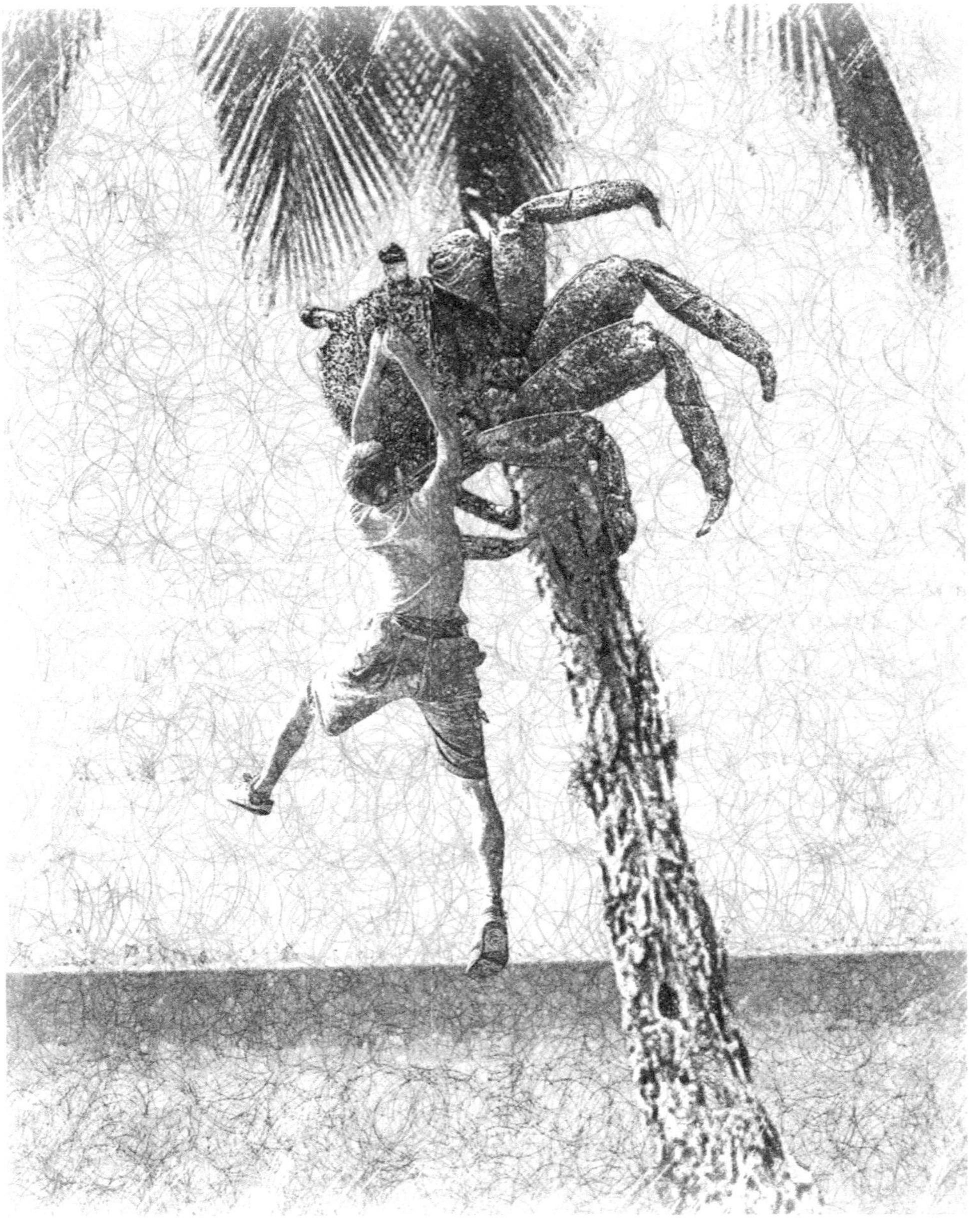

Axel angrily glared at Riqui.

"Now, now… relax, Axel. I'm positive you'll find what you are looking for." Hojo reassured him and with a small chuckle he said, "Come on. Let's go hunt for your seashells and weeds."

They left the house and hopped onto the boat. Hojo pointed to an area behind his house. "The trees in that part of the island are tallest. I love climbing' them trees and stayin' up there for hours."

Riqui paddled their transport toward those trees and parked it close to the tallest tree in that area. "Axel, I'm not going up there with you."

"How come?"

Hojo laughed. "He's a scaredy cat when it comes to heights. How about you, Axel, are you also scared?"

Axel pretended to ignore Hojo's question because he, too, was terrified of heights.

"Come on, hang on to my shoulder."

Axel moved closer to Hojo and put his arms on his shoulder.

"Hang on tight now." As soon as Hojo hopped onto the tree, he shifted into a crab, which made Axel almost fall. He pushed himself up to tighten his grip, but the rest of his body just dangled behind. With his claws and legs, Hojo started to climb up. Axel's heart started beating so fast, he kept his eyes closed all the way to the top of the tree.

"We're here. You can open your eyes now." Hojo shifted back to human form and helped Axel settle at the top.

Despite his unease, Axel gasped in awe. Here at the top of the highest tree, he felt like he was on top of the world. He could see the ocean waves splash onto the beach. Looking around, he viewed most of the island. From afar, he even saw the mainland, where the castle mountain was standing high with some hills around it. "Wow, Hojo, this view is amazing."

He saw crab people going about their own business. Some were building houses and some were making arts and crafts near the shore. Children were playing, and couples walked by the seashore. Hojo gave him a nudge, "so do you see what you are looking for?"

"Not yet," he answered, slowly turning around, looking everywhere and at everything.

The western side of the island was quite deserted. The northern section looked like a business center, where there was a concentration of what looked like stores. He was almost ready to give up when he saw some weeds floating in an area that looked like a cove. "Hojo, that area over there, on the west side," he pointed to it, "is that a cave or something like that?"

"Yeah, it is, and as a matter of fact, I believe there are some coral reefs there."

"Great! Maybe that's where I should go."

Axel hopped onto Hojo's back, but his transformation was so abrupt that Axel lost his grip again. He clung to one of Hojo's legs, as they descended rapidly to the ground.

"Good grief, Hojo. I almost fell," Axel complained as he stood up shakily.

"But you did not. I had everything under control."

"Right," Axel retorted.

Riqui was sitting on the ground and laughing, as he watched their descent.

"I think Axel now knows where he needs to go," Hojo proclaimed.

"Where is it?"

"Crabston Cove. You remember that place, Riqui, it's where we used to play when we were younger."

"Of course, I know that place. Okay, we had best get going. Thanks so much, bud. I owe you one. Let's get together sometime."

Instead of shaking hands, Riqui and Hojo slapped each other's claws. Axel did not attempt to shake his hand or slap his claw. He thanked Hojo and just waved goodbye.

— Chapter 24 —

The Crabstone Cove

Axel and Riqui headed towards Crabstone Cove. It was not very far, so they got there in very little time. They saw a place where weeds were just floating around. They walked closer, skipping over puddles of water.

"Now what?" asked Riqui.

Annoyed, Axel answered. "I don't know, I'm just winging it. Why can't you help me look for it?"

"Well, for your information, I have no idea what the clue you got meant."

"You saw the chest, the shell, and the writings. How can you say you don't know what they mean?"

"Because, silly, those words were meant only for you to see and understand, of course."

"Right." Axel replied, as he scouted the area. "Those weeds are unusually long. Maybe there are some coral reefs underneath them."

"Let's go follow the weeds."

Axel looked around to see where they came from. He noticed that they sprouted everywhere, but some of them extended from a hollow structure. His instincts told him those were the weeds he needed to check out. He carefully treaded along the sides heading toward the entrance of what he then realized was a cave.

He hesitated outside until Riqui said, "So, are we just going to watch the weeds?"

"No, I was just thinking."

"Yeah, about what? Or let me guess, you were thinking it's really scary inside the cave, should I go in or not?"

"That's not it. Fine, let's go in."

They proceeded, making sure they did not step on the weeds. As they passed the entrance, they stood in place to adjust their eyes to the dimness of the cave. Axel looked around and saw that the stream of water outside flowed from the pond that was in the middle of the cave. Along the sides of the pond were rocks of different sizes.

"Look at the water. It gets deeper over there. C'mon." He pointed toward the center of the cave.

Riqui gestured with his hand. "After you."

Axel peered through weeds that covered the surface of the pond and saw several beautiful colored reefs. Underneath one of the reefs, there was an object that caught his eye. While focusing on the object, he did not notice that the weeds started moving towards them. Before the weeds could get him, Riqui grabbed Axel by the waist and pulled him back.

"Why did you do that?" Axel yelled, pushing Riqui away.

Riqui pointed, "Take a look at that."

Axel noticed the weeds coming closer to him and instantly moved back. "Why are they moving and… and why towards me?"

"Ummm… maybe they like you," Riqui answered with a grin.

They moved further back, and the weeds retracted back to the pond.

"I saw something in the coral reef, I think it's an oyster, a big one. That makes sense, don't you think? Oysters have pearls!" Axel said excitedly.

"Looks like it, but what would you do about the weeds? How can you get past them?"

Axel sat on a rock, thinking of what to do. When Riqui saw Axel's face light up, he said. "Aha, you got an idea."

"Riqui, are you strong enough to carry those rocks?"

"I don't know, let me try." Riqui gripped the biggest rock and lifted it up. "Is this what you mean?"

Axel nodded.

"So, what's your plan?"

"I'm going near the weeds, but not too close. When the weed starts to come to me, I'll run back. If it follows me, I'll grab the end of the weed and pull it out of the water. You lift up the boulder, and when I get past you, drop the rock on the weed, and then I'll tie it around the rock."

"Sounds like a plan, but how many weeds are we talking about here?"

"I don't know. We'll just have to take them on one at a time."

"This crazy idea of yours might just work. Go for it. I'll be ready with the rock."

Axel moved closer to the water and, sure enough, a weed started approaching him. When the weed was about three feet closer, Axel started to walk backwards, and the weed followed him. Axel hurriedly grabbed the end and pulled it back past Riqui, who was already ready and holding the rock. "Now," cried Axel, and Riqui dropped the rock on the weed. Axel wrapped the ends around the rock and tied it to itself.

Axel sat down, panting. "Looks like there are several weeds that need to be tied."

He got up and they both worked laboriously to do the same thing to the rest of the weeds that seemed to be protecting the thing inside the coral reef.

When the weeds were out of the way, Axel stepped in the water and went closer to the object. He smiled at Riqui and said, "I knew it was an oyster."

"How are you supposed to open the oyster?"

"I have no idea." On impulse, he knocked on the oyster. The oyster opened, and he saw something glittering inside.

Riqui tried to take a closer look. "Could be a pearl."

"I don't think so. Pearls are roundish. It looks like two pieces. That's it, I found it," Axel said excitedly. He was about to grab the gems, but the oyster closed. "No, no, no. Don't do that to me. After all the hard work, you need to let me have it."

Axel pounded on the oyster again, but the oyster did not open. Axel went back to the ground and sat down. He did not know what to do. "I've come this far I can't stop now. Riqui, please push one of those rocks to the water and come with me."

Riqui pushed a rock, and Axel pulled it over the water toward the oyster. He again knocked on the oyster, but the oyster did not open. "Riqui, can you pry this oyster open? When it opens, I'll put the rock inside to keep it open."

Riqui tried to pry open the oyster with his claws, but the oyster would not open. He saw the weeds starting to wiggle free.

"What am I supposed to do, Riqui?"

After staring at the oyster for a while, Axel noticed that it had started to open. An immediate impulse propelled him to push the rock inside it, which accidentally made him fall in the water. A smile glowed on his face despite his body being soaked. The rock kept the oyster open, and Axel rushed to grab the two gems inside.

Axel put the gems in his pant pocket. As he turned around to step out of the pond, he stopped to look back. Seeing the rock inside the oyster, a sense of guilt crept over him. He reached over to pry out the rock. The oyster snapped shut, almost catching Axel's hand. He rubbed his hand thankfully, imagining his hand could have been chopped off.

"Riqui, let's release the weeds." Axel untied, one and Riqui lifted the rock. The weed immediately returned to the water. One by one, they freed each plant until they all settled next to the oyster again.

Outside of the cave, Riqui said, "Congratulations, Axel. You succeeded with your first challenge. You got our tribe's treasure."

"So now what am I supposed to do with them?"

"Crabs are known for speed. We can travel at super speed if we need to, though of course, a few special ones are faster than others. From what I've heard, those celestial gems can give you the ability to move fast but only if you are bonded with them."

"Really? How fast can you go?" Axel excitedly asked.

"Well, I can show you."

Riqui shifted to his crab form and sped away from Axel. In a short while, he was back beside Axel.

"So, where did you go?"

"I just traveled around the island. I can go even faster if I want to."

"How do I know you really ran around the island? I didn't see you."

"You're such a skeptic. Come on, hop on my back."

"You mean now?"

"Yeah, so you can see and feel for yourself, silly."

Axel hopped on his back.

"Hang on tight. You wouldn't want to fly off," Riqui warned. This time, he did not change into a crab.

Axel got worried. "Can you still be as fast even if you remain in human form?"

"Certainly, so hang on." Axel tightened his grip, and Riqui signaled, "Three, two, one," and sped away.

Before Axel was able to speak, they were back where they came from. "Good grief. That was incredible!"

"Well then, that will be great when you can acquire this ability. It may take some time, but I believe in you, and with a lot of practice, I trust you will be able to go as fast as I can." Riqui took out a small, circular object from his pocket. He pressed it, and in an instant, his blue mini jet appeared.

"You have a jet, too?" Axel asked in surprise.

"Of course." He grinned and patted Axel on the shoulder. When the jet opened, Axel had to squeeze himself because Riqui's jet was much smaller than Ujin's. When both were settled inside, Riqui started the engine, then flew at super speed back to the castle.

— CHAPTER 25 —

Bonding with the Cancer Gem

Riqui parked his jet in one of the open spaces. They both exited the vehicle and proceeded to enter the closest circular structure that whirled them up. Upon reaching the queen's chambers, Ujin and the queen greeted them with a round of applause. Isyna was also present but nonchalantly stood to the side.

Riqui and Axel bowed to the queen.

"Congratulations, Axel. I am so proud of you," the queen said.

Ujin shook Riqui's hand. "Thank you for helping Axel with his first challenge"

"Did you have a hard time?" the queen asked.

"Yes, I did," Axel replied honestly, as he pulled the gem from his pocket and showed it to the queen. There were two similar pieces that interlocked. They were attracted to each other by a magnetic force but could be separated when pulled apart.

"Hold on to it first. This is truly exciting." She was so elated that she clapped her hands. "In appreciation of what you have achieved today, we are going to have a feast. Let us all head to the dining room. You must be tired and hungry."

Both Axel and Riqui nodded, as they followed the Queen, Ujin, and Isyna. The dining table was already prepared, and Johan and his three assistants were waiting to serve them. They laid the dishes on each plate and poured their drinks.

Axel stared at the food, as they were not the burgers and fries that were served to him before.

The Queen saw Axel's reaction and smiled. "These are our native dishes. I hope you enjoy them."

They all quietly started to eat except for Axel who hesitated at first. Not wanting to disrespect the queen, he scooped a piece of what looked like meat and surprisingly, he liked the taste. It was even more astonishing that he was able to finish all the food on his plate.

After the restful break, Queen Elyjanah announced, "Axel, the next step is for you to bond with the crystal gems."

"Your Majesty, do you still need me?" Riqui interrupted. "If not, I would like to head back home."

"Of course, you may go, Riqui, and thank you for a job well done."

Riqui bowed and left the queen's room.

Queen Elyjanah and Axel entered the sacred room. She instructed Axel, "Step up, take your shoes off, and reach for the belt. To bond with the gems, you need to absorb the energy from them."

"How do I do that?"

"Once you're wearing the belt, put one gem on each foot. The transference should occur at that point, and the process will take its own course. Just like before, don't panic and just relax. Do you have any questions?"

"Do I have a choice?"

"At this time, no, but believe in yourself. You'll be fine. Are you ready?"

"Not really."

Queen Elyjanah patted his shoulder, turned, and exited the sacred room.

Reluctantly, Axel took off his shoes and touched the belt. It uncoiled and wrapped around his waist. Axel placed one celestial gem on top of each foot. As the gems emitted a surge of energy, he felt a sharp pain in his feet. His heart started pounding faster and faster. He started panicking, and his instincts told him to escape, but Queen Elyjanah's voice filled his mind. He took a deep breath, closed his eyes, and focused to calm his nerves.

The energy from the gems gradually crept upward until it reached the belt, and at this point of contact, it started radiating a light that filled the room. Thinking that he was about to explode, that this was his end, and that he was never going to see his family, friends, and home again, Axel started crying.

It seemed like this was eternity, but the process took only a few minutes. The bright light slowly dimmed until it completely faded. Axel looked down at his feet, but the gems were no longer there. He touched the belt all around his waist and felt something strange. Looking down, he was surprised to see the gems attached to the image that matched the figures. Axel moved away from the pedestal and exited the room.

Queen Elyjanah and Ujin were outside, anxiously waiting for him. Happy to see Axel, she exclaimed, "Congratulations, you have bonded with the first of the twelve celestial gems!"

Axel felt wobbly but tried to balance himself with each stride. "What happens now?"

"Compared to all other inhabitants in our world, Cancers have the heightened ability of speed, some greater than others of course. Bonding with their sacred gem gave you this ability as well," the queen explained.

"Wow, can I go as fast as Riqui?"

Queen Elyjanah raised her right brow and then smiled. "A bit impatient, aren't you? Just rest for now and have a drink of water." She handed Axel a glass. "The power of speed that I'm talking about is not just running fast. It also involves speed in action or tasks performed. However, even though you have bonded, it will still take time to fully master this ability. You may or may not achieve its full potential. It all depends on your resolve."

"How do you feel now?" Ujin asked.

Stretching his arms and legs, he answered, "I think I'm okay."

"Well then, why don't you give it a try? The hallway ramp is long enough to run through. Ujin, how about showing him how to start?"

"As you wish, Your Majesty." Ujin opened the door that led to the ramp. "Axel, position your body like you are about to run a race, like this." Ujin modeled the position. "Take a deep breath, take off, and run. Make sure you maintain your balance—that's the key to your speed. Be careful. The ramp is inclined, so you'll need to adjust your pace to run downwards and upwards."

Axel positioned his body the way Ujin showed him. "Like this?"

Ujin nodded.

"This should be easy. I like running." Then he took off but with the third step forward, he tripped, fell, and rolled over. "Ouch!" he cried.

The queen tried not to laugh.

Ujin had no such qualms. He roared with laughter. "You're such a dummy."

"You just told me to get into position and then run," Axel retorted as he stood up.

"Okay, fine. Straighten your body, jog in place, and slowly move forward. As you move ahead, get into a rhythm. Once you feel that you are in control of your pace, gradually increase your speed. How fast you can go depends on your balance. Try it again."

This time, Axel did as he was instructed. He started jogging in place and then moved forward to run through the ramp. He went faster and faster. It seemed like it was just a minute before he reached the bottom of the mountain and then ran back up. "How fast did I go?"

"Umm, it was okay."

"Okay? Just, okay?" Axel frowned then turned around to try again. He repeated the rhythmic jog in place and sped ahead. His confidence was so overwhelming that he did not notice the foot that blocked his path on the fifth level. With that mishap, he tumbled down several steps, knocked his head on the railing, and fell unconscious.

The queen gasped, and Ujin ran to check on Axel.

"Oops, sorry about that," Isyna said, trying to hide her smile.

Her mother stared angrily but refrained from reprimanding her. At that moment, she was more concerned with Axel.

Ujin carried Axel back to the queen's chamber and laid him on the couch.

Queen Elyjanah used her healing powers to help him regain consciousness. "How are you feeling, Axel?" she asked.

"I guess I'm okay," he said, trying to sit up. "I want to go home now."

"Of course."

Without needing a reminder, Axel returned the belt to the sacred room. The queen said, "Goodbye, Axel. Until next time, take care of yourself."

With that said, the queen summoned her daughter.

Isyna stepped into the room and started the conversation. "I know you are upset over what I did to Axel." She shrugged. "It was an accident. I did not know he was running down. Besides, that proves he has not gotten the power of speed, right? He may not be the chosen one after all." Isyna tried to seem confident but felt uneasy under the pressure of her mother's stern gaze.

"I am very upset with the stunt you pulled on Axel. You know perfectly well the danger we are facing. Being just a kid, Axel has been plunged into a difficult predicament. Chosen or not, I expect you never to make the same mistake again and give him your full support. Is that understood, Isyna?"

Feeling defeated and fighting her tears, she softly said, "Yes, mom."

Out in the hall, Axel formed the portal with the ring.

Ujin tried to comfort him. "Get lots of rest and, if needed, see a physician for a checkup. Take care of yourself."

"I always do," he shouted, as he was sucked into the tunnel, landing back in this room and on his bed without a problem.

Exhaustion caused him to immediately doze off until he was awakened by Christa, who burst into his bedroom.

"Axel's got a girlfriend. Axel's got a girlfriend," she chanted.

"What are you talking about?" he asked, annoyed and rubbing his eyes.

"There's a Rena in our living room asking for you."

Axel jumped out of bed and sprinted to the bathroom, pushing Christa out of the way.

"Watch where you're going, you dork!" Christa yelled.

He was so excited to see Rena again.

When Rena saw him, she smiled. "Hi, Axel, are you feeling better?"

Remembering that he asked to go home because of a headache, he nodded. "Yeah, I'm better now. Thanks."

"I came here to give you a copy of our assignments."

"When do we have to submit them?"

"Math is tomorrow, but the essay is on Monday."

"Thanks, Rena. You're the best."

Sarah came out with some snacks and lemonade. "Here you go, some snacks for you."

"You didn't have to but thanks, Mrs. Knight."

After they ate the snack, Rena and Axel took the plate back to the kitchen, and Axel walked Rena home before dark.

— CHAPTER 26 —

A New Enemy

In a distant land beyond the great desert of the outer realm, residing in a camp was a squad of militant cheetahs. They were part of the Taurus tribe who were known for their aggressiveness and speed, much like the ability of the Cancer Tribe. This base half-way up a mountain was well-fortified and fully equipped with an arsenal of weapons and tanks. Warriors inside the fortress were continuously exercising and practicing their combat maneuvers. Commander Dulli was the head of the infantry, and he imposed strict discipline.

It was an unusually hot day, as Commander Dulli paced back and forth from his desk to the window. Because his office faced the desert, it was hotter than any other room in the building. He did not mind the heat because it made him feel strong and aggressive, which in his mind, were the essential characteristics of a great leader. Also, he was paranoid about enemies invading his camp. He considered his office the watch tower.

This military base had been built to protect their lands from invaders, but Commander Dulli had a secret, sinister goal: he wanted to steal the celestial gem of the Taurus tribe. Failure was unforgivable. It was Commander Dulli's responsibility to assure the success of this goal, but he was extremely frustrated with the slow progress of their operation. His anger was totally focused on Noby, to whom he had given the special assignment of infiltrating the tribe, especially their enemy's law enforcement agency.

"Noby, why don't you have any info on the gems yet? It's been more than a year now, and we got nothing," Dulli yelled.

"I've tried to blend with the people. I rented a house and opened a business to get to know as many Taurus citizens as I could. No one seemed to know about those gems."

"Yeah, I know that already. What else is new?"

"Recently, I came across an old teacher named Patkijn Liim. He told me something that may be important. I befriended him, but it took a long time to gain his trust. I even enrolled in his history class! For weeks, I followed him until he agreed to be my mentor. When I asked about the gem, he became suspicious of my intentions. I felt he discarded his doubts when I explained the importance of this myth in my fictional story."

"So, what did he say?"

"He said he was not sure, but he thinks that only the chief elder, Tiroh, knows where the gems are hidden."

"Then why didn't you make the chief talk?"

"It's not that easy. He does not allow strangers in his house or even in his office. There may be a way, but I'm not sure it's a good idea. Taurus creatures are very strong, much stronger than we are, so it may be hard to do."

"Speak up. What's your idea?"

"Tiroh has a daughter named Amora. We can kidnap her and demand Tiroh for the gem as ransom."

"Hmmmm... not bad... not bad at all."

"I do not exactly have a plan yet. I've never even seen Amora, so I don't know what she looks like."

Dulli transformed into an angry cheetah, grabbed the front of Noby's shirt with his paw, and lifted him against the wall. "I don't care about what you do or do not know!" he roared. "Just go do what you need to do to get the gems, or I'll exile you to limbo; better yet, I'll break all your bones!"

Choking, Noby answered, "Yes, sir."

At that moment, both Dulli and Noby heard an eerie sound emanating from the opposite direction. Both turned their heads, looking for the source. Dulli dropped Noby and returned to his human form—a frightful image of Sevion had appeared in the room.

Dulli and Noby knelt and bowed down to his image.

"Greetings, Lord Sevion. What can we do for you?" Commander Dulli asked nervously.

Noby kept his head down.

Sevion glared at Dulli. When he spoke, his voice had an eerie whisper to it. "I understand you have not yet stolen the Taurus gem. Why not?"

"Well, I assigned Noby this task. He acquired information that will help, but so far, he had not made any progress. We were just discussing a new plan to acquire the gem."

Sevion turned his stern gaze to Noby. "Are you sure your plan will work?"

"I will do my best," Noby said with a quivering voice.

"Very well. I expect to have that gem in my hands in three days. If I don't receive it, you both know the punishment awaiting you."

"Yes, Lord Sevion," they responded.

Sevion's image started to fade away.

Noby breathed a sigh of relief, but Dulli transformed back into a cheetah to attack him.

Noby tried to block Dulli. "Please, sir, I understand the urgency of this task! I meant what I said to Lord Savion. I will do my best."

"Fine," Dulli said, sitting on the couch to relax. He was extremely stressed by Sevion.

After giving him a salute, Noby left and returned to his house, which was on the outskirts of Taurus mainland. On his way home, his mind was filled with thoughts of different scenarios to complete his mission.

Noby's meeting with Commander Dulli drained all his energy, so he sank into his bed and fell asleep. Later, he was awakened by vehicles honking on the road, a normal occurrence at this time in the afternoon. The first thing he did when he got up was to get an alcoholic drink. He looked out the window to see the traffic and sighed, shaking his head.

He shivered at the thought of the Sevion's punishment if he ever failed. He sipped his drink and started pacing back and forth, thinking of what to do. He really had no idea how to begin the new strategy, much less how to make a real plan for it. Frustrated, he decided to go deeper into the Taurus mainland.

Just as he had done each time he traveled to the Taurus territory, he put on one of his many disguises. He masqueraded as a painter, a barber, a merchant, a race car driver, a student and even an old crazy man, depending on the situation. For this trip, because he decided to talk to Patkijn Liim, he disguised himself as a student again.

When he was all dressed for the plan, he rode his jet all the way to his other apartment in the downtown area of the region. He dropped off his luggage and proceeded directly to the library, where the teacher spent most of his free time.

Noby looked around as he stepped inside the library, hoping he would easily spot the teacher. To his dismay, he was nowhere in sight. Anxious, Noby headed to his mentor's office.

On the way, he kept thinking how uncertain this plan was, but for fear of Commander Dulli's threats, he had to cling to the hope that this step would lead to fulfilling his duty and special assignment.

He knocked on the door, and the teacher called for him to enter. Noby was so thankful hearing the teacher's voice that he put his hand on his chest and breathed a sigh of relief.

— Chapter 27 —

Danger Ahead

For the first time since he stepped foot on Zycodia, Axel felt a sense of accomplishment and thought he may really be the chosen one. Finding the Cancer tribe's celestial gem and bonding with it was, indeed, a job well done, yet he clung to the distant hope that someone else could fulfill this destiny. Weeks went by. School was good, and his friendship with Rena continued. They studied, researched, and worked on projects together.

Rena was not into musical instruments. Instead, she joined the choir at the beginning of the year. She had a beautiful soprano voice and often landed solos in the school performances. Of course, Axel was her number one fan.

Axel submitted all his essays and assignments on time and was quite content by how his review for upcoming tests was going along. He was almost done with his last review when suddenly he felt his hand start to sting.

He groaned, frustrated at the possibility of missing the tests for which he had studied so hard, yet with the increasing throbbing pain in his hand, he didn't have the option of ignoring the call.

As upset as he was, his consolation was that because it was Friday, there was still time to come back before the test the following week. He put on the ring and wrapped the sash around his waist. He took a backpack from his closet and filled it with a couple snacks, a juice box, his journal and a pen Before he touched the tapestry, he pulled his bed closer to the wall, so he could land on it when he returned.

Even after a few trips through the tunnel, he was still not used to the feeling of being suctioned through it. At times, he felt out of breath, even nauseated. The landings, which were unpredictable, were the most painful of all.

"Here I go again." Axel took a deep breath and placed his hand on the tapestry. In a flash, he was whirled through the tunnel. This time, Axel landed on the fifth level, where the twelve doors were located. Ujin was there to greet him.

"Hello again, Axel," Ujin said with a smile on this face, as he helped Axel get up.

"Hi Ujin. Why was I called back here again, and why are you smiling?"

"I can smile too, you know. It's good to see you back. Anyway, Queen Elyjanah summoned you because of an imminent danger in one of our tribal communities."

"What tribe? How does she know about the danger?"

"As I told you before, Queen Elyjanah has the gift of foresight. Actually, Isyna does, too. It is in their royal blood. Anyway, she said that the daughter of the Taurus chief is in danger. Our enemies are obsessed with getting all our celestial gems because doing so would give them the ability to conquer our world. My guess is that their intention is to kidnap the daughter and demand the crystal treasures as a ransom."

"Does anyone in that tribe know about this danger?" Axel asked.

"Not yet. That's why it's imperative for us to go to Chief Tiroh and warn him of this danger. He already knows about you and your mission, so when we get there, we'll just ask for his help to find the gem. If we get it on time, we may be able to save his daughter from being kidnapped."

"Let's go see the queen."

Ujin and Axel rode up the elevator. The queen met them in front of her chambers and smiled. "Hello Axel. How are you?"

"I'm good."

"Ujin, did you explain the situation to Axel?"

"Yes, I did, Your Majesty."

"So, Axel, did you bring your sash with you?" she asked.

"Yes, I did."

"Remember, from now on, you must wear the belt when needed."

They both went to the sacred room, but before Axel extended his hand to touch the belt, it uncoiled and wrapped around Axel's waist. "Whoa!"

The queen smiled. "You and the belt now belong together. Put the sash over the belt before you leave. Good luck."

Ujin and Axel bowed and left the chamber. They went back to the fifth level where there were doors set in a circular pattern. Looking at the symbols on the doors, he pointed. "Is that the room we should enter?"

Ujin nodded and led Axel through the door.

— CHAPTER 28 —

The Next Challenge

Very little light illuminated the room. Through the darkness, Axel saw a statue of a bull under the corner lamp. Huge chairs were lined up against the walnut-colored walls. Horns hung on the walls as decorations. Every decoration in the room seemed massive.

They walked across the room towards the opposite exit door, where Ujin's jet was all set and ready to go.

Axel was still looking back at the room when Ujin yelled, "Axel, hurry up. There's no time to waste."

He dashed to the jet. With super speed, it darted through the tunnel and in a flash, they were hovering in a place quite different from the land of the Cancers. Through the transparent jet, he saw massive houses with huge doors and windows. The roads were wide and paved with dark cobblestones. Tall trees lined the roadsides. The parked vehicles were mostly bigger than those he saw before.

"Is this the Taurus land?"

"Yes."

"What kind of people are they?

"You'll find out soon enough," Ujin replied, as he landed in front of an elegant house. They got out of the Swifty and walked to the front door.

Like in the Cancer tribe, the chief official of the Taurus tribe lived in the center of their land. His home stood on top of a hill. To his estimate, the chief's house was the biggest in the land. The ground walkway in front was covered with dark bricks. Propped in the middle of the lawn was a massive fountain surrounded by well-trimmed bushes.

Upon reaching the enormous front door, Ujin knocked using the big, brass ring. They waited for several minutes until a man wearing what appeared to be a butler uniform opened the door.

"How may I help you, sir?" he asked.

Ujin frowned. "I've never seen you before. Are you new here?"

The butler nodded. "I'm here to replace the previous butler, who had fallen ill."

"Well, we are here to see Chief Tiroh."

"May I ask what for?"

"Please tell him that Ujin is here with a friend."

"Come in. Have a seat, sir, and I will let him know you are here."

Ujin and Axel sat down on a huge couch.

Axel whispered to Ujin, "His house is *massive*."

Before Ujin could answer, the butler came back and said, "The chief will see you now. Please follow me." When the butler opened another huge door, they saw a big bull lounging in a plush chair fit for his size. Behind him was a huge portrait, which Axel suspected was a safe to hide valuables. He was wearing a velvet red robe and fluffy slippers. His hind legs were crossed but his front legs, or arms, were on the armrests. His right hand still in human form was holding a cigar, and his left hand was holding a wine class

Axel thought it was really a very funny sight but hid his amusement.

"Ahhhh, Ujin, please come in. Thank you, Thom. Close the door on your way out." As Tiroh stood up, he transformed into a human figure and shook Ujin's hand.

"Is Thom your new butler? Where is your old butler?" Ujin asked.

"I don't know. One day, he just didn't come to work. We thought he was sick, so I had our police department look for him, but he was nowhere to be found. Even now, no one knows where he is. I had to hire a new butler. He came highly recommended."

Ujin nodded as he listened then changed the topic. "Is it true one of your prisoners escaped? How did it happen?

"His name is Digan. We have been investigating, and until now, we have no lead as to where he is hiding. He will be in big trouble once I catch him again!" Tiroh glanced at Axel and waved his hand. "Enough of that. Let's discuss our business."

Ujin cleared his throat. "This is Axel, the one we talked about during our last meeting."

"I see." With an aristocratic flare, he sat down on his lounging chair again, sipped his drink, and signaled for them to sit in the visitor chairs.

Axel felt dwarfed by the huge chair.

"So, this is the Axel I've been hearing about, the so-called Chosen One. Well then, Axel, how does it feel to be chosen by destiny?"

Axel snorted. "Truth is, I wish I was not the one."

Chief Tiroh straightened up in his seat and seemed intrigued. "Ahhh, a skeptic!" He glanced at Ujin then continued. "Anyway, you do know that you have to pass a test before you get our treasure, yes?"

With a frown, Axel answered, "So I have been told several times."

Suddenly, the door opened and in came a... cow? Axel blinked. It was wearing a pink gown. It walked closer to Axel and started sniffing him all over. Axel jolted up from the chair and moved away from the cow.

"Stop it!" he yelled.

Tiroh laughed but in a commanding voice said, "Stop it, Amora." He approached the cow and pulled its front legs up. "This is my beautiful daughter. Come on, Amora."

She shifted into her human form, young and about Axel's age. She had short brown hair, black eyes, and deep-set dimples. She had a well-proportioned body and a brownish complexion.

"You know Ujin, our chief defense minister and the queen's personal counselor, right? This is Axel, Ujin's new trainee."

Axel was surprised by how pretty she was.

"Are you staying with us?" she asked.

"No," Ujin said. "We are just visiting your dad, and I'll just be showing Axel your land."

"Nice. Can I go with them, dad?"

"No, Amora. Go do your homework."

"Darn, that's no fun."

"How about playing a musical piece for our guests before you go?"

"All right, as long as I can go with them."

With a remote control from his desk, the chief pressed some buttons that automatically opened a sliding door, revealing a room that had musical instruments, a projector, and chairs lined up against the walls. One would guess this was like an entertainment room for guests.

He walked in and signaled everyone to enter the room. They all sat on the chairs while Amora sat on a stool in front of an instrument that Axel thought was a piano. As she started to play, it sounded more like a harp ... a somber yet seemingly hopeful melody filled the room. They were all swept with sentimental emotions, especially Axel.

When Amora finished playing her piece, Axel exclaimed, "That was beautiful."

"Thank you." She then stood up, shifted into a cow figure again and rubbed her nose on Axel's chest. Axel was about to jump up when Amora turned around and left the room.

"Well then. Let's go back to my office." Tiroh said, leading the way. "Where were we?"

"We were talking about the challenge, or rather, the test," Ujin answered.

"Oh, yes." Tiroh strode to the end of the room and locked his office door. "We can never be too careful, you know."

Behind his desk, there was a huge painting of a bull hung on the wall above a long credenza. He pulled a lock and opened it like a cabinet door, exposing what Axel thought was a safe to hide important things.

The smile from Axel's face caught Tiroh's eyes. "What are you smiling about?"

"It's just that I guessed that behind that painting was a safe."

"You guessed right."

Axel curiously watched as Tiroh placed his hand on a panel which automatically opened the metallic safe. He peeped inside and was surprised to see an empty space. Tiroh put his hand inside and pulled out a scroll.

"There was nothing inside!" Axel exclaimed.

"Really, now? So what's this in my hand?" He removed the ribbon to unroll it and then handed it to Ujin, who, after studying the contents, passed it on to Axel.

Looking at the scroll, Axel said, "I don't know what this means."

"Oh, I forgot you can't read our tongue." Tiroh waved his hand over the scroll, and the symbols transformed into words that Axel was able to read.

In plain sight, a stone
Untouched by time,
Embrace its beauty to own
The might of nine.

Axel wrote the riddle in his journal and handed the scroll back to the chief.

"So, Axel, do you think you can figure out what that means?"

He scratched his head. "I've got no clue at all."

"Thank you for your help." Ujin shook the chief's hand, as they headed to the door. "We will come back to see you when Axel's task is done."

"It was my pleasure. Good luck, Axel."

"Thank you," he replied.

Ujin reached for the doorknob, but before he could open it, Amora burst inside. She was dressed in a full jumpsuit, rubber shoes, gloves, a hat, and had hung a bag over her shoulder.

"I'm ready!" she excitedly announced.

Ujin and Axel gave each other a wide-eyed glance.

"Where do you think you're going?" Tiroh angrily said.

"I'm going with them. I know what they're up to, and I want to join the fun adventure!"

"No, you're not going anywhere. What about your studies?"

"I've done them, so I'm going."

"No, you're not," Tiroh said in a scolding manner.

"Yes, I am," she said, stomping out of the room.

"She really is so stubborn." Tiroh sighed. "I guess she got that trait from me, so I understand where she's coming from. Very well, take her with you. She is smart. She really may be able to help you."

As they were walking toward the front door, Axel noticed that the new butler seemed to jump from where he was sitting in the hallway. He looked edgy but still bowed and turned away.

Strange dude, Axel thought as they left the house.

— CHAPTER 29 —

The Elusive Stone

"What took you so long?" Amora asked Ujin and Axel when they stepped outside.

She was leaning on the weirdest looking bike Axel had ever seen. It was huge. It looked like a motorcycle with four thrusters mounted on each side of the wheels.

Ujin said to Axel, "Since Amora is going with you, I'll head back to the castle, but I will check on you now and then. You do know that your translator can also be used as a communication device, right? Press the right button, and I'll answer." Ujin turned to Amora. "I need to go back to the castle. Do you mind if I leave Axel with you?"

"No prob. This will be fun." She smiled at Axel. "Hop on my bike! It seats two."

Axel sat behind Amora, and off she sped down the street.

"Whoa, Amora, stop, stop, would you stop for a minute?" he yelled. "We don't even know where to go."

In a flash, Amora stepped hard on the brakes, and they skidded to a complete stop. Axel was almost thrown off with the forward jerk. Amora parked in front of what looked like a restaurant. She pranced toward the building. Axel followed. He was surprised to see several bulls dining inside. At the massive counter, Amora placed an order.

"Do you want something to eat?"

"No, thank you. I brought some snacks. Besides I'm not hungry yet."

A gallon of something was handed to Amora. She led the way to an empty table at the far end of the dining area. No one was in that section but them.

"What's in that big container?"

"Oh, it's a frozen dessert, like your ice cream. Want some?"

Shaking his head, he asked, "Can you really finish all of that?"

"Just watch me!"

While Amora ate her snack, he looked around trying to absorb everything and everyone he saw. He noticed a wanted poster pinned on the store's bulletin board. "Is this the prisoner, Digan, that your dad told us about?" he asked, gesturing at the poster.

"Yup."

Axel took out his journal and read the riddle again.

"What are you reading?" She curiously took a peep at it, but Axel instinctively closed his journal.

"It's something that they said can help me find what I'm looking for."

"Oh, don't be so secretive. I know that you are looking for our celestial gem, right? My dad told me about it."

"Shh, quiet. Someone might hear you."

"I know. I know. It's supposed to be a secret; but I'm here to help you, aren't I? So, spit it out."

"Fine." He opened his journal and recited the riddle to Amora. *"In plain sight, a stone untouched by time, embrace its beauty to own, the might of nine."*

"Do you have any idea what it means, Axel?"

"If I did, I wouldn't need any help, would I?" He sighed. "Got no clue. Although, from my previous challenge, I had to start thinking of the riddle in the simplest way, which is to think of its meaning literally. So, if I follow the same line of thought, we should be looking for a stone, but what kind of stone and where it could be is the problem."

"I'm done eating. Let's go." Amora exclaimed.

"Wow, you really *did* finish the entire bucket."

"Yeah, yeah, I was hungry."

"So, where to?"

"I don't know. Maybe we should just drive around and see if something catches our eyes, Amora."

"Okay, better than doing nothing."

Off they rode through the streets of the Taurus land. First, they went to an area with entertainment centers, archives, and different buildings much like downtown on earth cities. Then, they went toward houses which were mostly aristocratic. They passed by hillsides and parks. They practically toured the entire community that afternoon, but they saw no stone.

After a couple of hours, it started to get dark, so they headed back to Amora's house. When they got back, Axel sat on the big couch in the receiving room. He pressed his communicator and called Ujin.

He answered right away. "Yes, Axel. How is it going? Have you found it?"

"No, not yet, but it's getting dark. I want to go home."

"I'll be right there."

Axel relaxed on the couch and closed his eyes to rest. It wasn't long before Ujin arrived at Chief Tiroh's house. The butler let him in. Axel looked at the butler and somehow, he still had that strange feeling about him. Unable to understand his reaction, he decided to ignore it for the moment.

Chief Tiroh entered the receiving room with Amora, who had already changed her outfit. The chief greeted them both then turned to Axel. "So, did you find what you were looking for?"

"No, not yet, sir."

"It's nighttime already. Why don't you stay here for the night?"

"Thank you, but I prefer to go home. I have to study for my tests on Monday."

"Okay then. When will you come back?"

"As soon as I can. Goodbye, sir. Amora, thank you for your help today."

"No biggie," she said. "It was fun. We'll do it again when you come back."

Ujin and Axel rode the Swiftie back to the castle. The queen knew Axel did not have the celestial gem. She said, "I know you want to go home, so just return the belt to the sacred room." Axel went inside the sanctuary chamber to return the belt. After the belt settled in its place, Axel left the room and said goodbye to the queen and Ujin.

"Come back as soon as possible, Axel. Remember, Amora's life is in danger."

Axel nodded and opened the portal to go back home.

— CHAPTER 30 —

In Plain Sight

Axel zoomed through the tunnel and, in a few seconds, popped out of the tapestry. Just as he fell onto his bed, his mom opened the door.

"Axel, your dad needs a hand with what he is doing. Go and help him, will you? He is outside."

"Why is he working at home? It's Friday night."

"He is doing it for a friend. So, go on and help him."

He stepped outside. "Hi dad, mom said you needed help."

Charles looked up from under the hood of the four-door sedan he was fixing. "Good, you're here. Yeah, go inside the car and open the window. Step on the brake when I tell you to."

"'Kay," Axel answered as he got in position.

Charles moved to the back of the car and said, "Now, Axel."

Axel stepped on the brake.

"Good. Press the right turn signal."

With a nod, he turned and flipped the switch to the right.

"Now do the same for the left turn signal."

Axel did so.

"That's good. Thanks."

As the sun dropped below the horizon, they heard Sarah call them both for supper. It was wonderful to eat his mom's cooking. Axel was still holding onto the hope the other world didn't exist and that everything that had happened so far was just a bad dream. Amora and the day they spent together preoccupied his thoughts. Although their trip was unproductive, he had a good time. Amora was fun to be with. He did not realize the smile that had formed on his face.

"Earth to Axel." Christa punched his arm. "Dad's talking to you. What are you smiling about?" She rolled her eyes. "Oh, I know. He's thinking about his girlfriend."

"What girlfriend?" Charles asked.

"Rena, isn't that her name?" Christa grinned at Axel.

"She's not my girlfriend. She is a very close friend and classmate."

Charles broke off the conversation. "Axel, I'm going to need your help tomorrow morning."

"What for, dad?"

"I have to pick up a car from the other side of town."

"It's the weekend, why do you have to work?"

"The owner said his car needs to be repaired, but he has no time to bring it to the shop. Says he won't give his car to anyone but me for repair. I've fixed it before. Remember Vic?"

Axel nodded as he continued to eat.

After the scrumptious meal, Axel returned to his room with one goal in mind: to finish reviewing for his tests in case he had to leave in a hurry. He finished studying in about three hours, then took a bath and went to bed. Up until he fell asleep, his mind was plagued with the riddle. *In plain sight, a stone untouched...*

As dawn broke, Charles woke Axel up for their trip to Vic's house. On the way, Axel asked his dad, "What's wrong with his car?"

"It won't start. My guess is the starter; but can't be sure until I see the car. Vic also wants me to check the brakes and change the oil… basically do an overall checkup."

"That's a lot to work on."

"Oh, nothing out of the ordinary," Charles said as he slowed down to a stop. "We're here."

Charles got out of the car, walked through the driveway and knocked on the front door of Vic's huge, two-story house.

Vic greeted him with a big, seemingly grateful smile. "Thanks for coming. I love that car, but it drives me nuts when something goes wrong with it. I have meetings today that I can't miss. That's why I really, really appreciate you taking the time to come over."

Vic stepped out of the house and led Charles to the car. He removed the items that he needed and handed over the keys.

"How long before I can get the car back?"

"I'll call you once I've inspected it and give you a quote and time estimate."

"Sounds good." They shook hands and, Vic went back to the house.

After putting the car in neutral, Charles and Axel pushed the car out of the driveway. To tow the car, the chain was attached to the truck's latch. When the car was safely connected, Charles and Axel headed back home.

It was almost lunchtime when Charles parked his truck along the side of the road. He unhooked the latch, and they pushed the car to the warehouse within their property.

They had lunch before Charles started working on Vic's car. He did a quick survey of the fluids and the starter, then performed a detailed check of the entire engine.

"Axel, would you go to the workshop and get my socket wrench box? You know what it looks like, right?" Charles gave Axel the key to the storage room in the warehouse.

Axel nodded and walked to the storage room. He opened the door and looked from left to right. The walls were lined with shelves which held a variety of tools, small gadgets, slabs of wood and other things that Axel couldn't identify. He searched through each shelf about three times but was not able to find the box. He went back to his dad and said, "Dad, I did not see a socket wrench box anywhere. I looked all around the place several times."

Charles raised his head out of the hood. "It's on the worktable. It's just in plain sight. Go again."

Axel went back to the storage room. Remembering what his dad said... *it's on the table... just in plain sight,* Axel looked closely at the worktable and there next to the hardware organizer was the see-through box *in plain sight.*

"In plain sight," he repeated and suddenly smiled. An idea sparked in his mind. It was as if a light bulb had been turned on in a dark room. He took the box, locked up the workshop, and gave it to his dad. "Are you still going to need me? If not, I have things to do."

"That will be all for today. Thanks, Axel"

Excited with this new thought, Axel went to his room, got the ring, sash and communicator. He packed some snacks, his glasses, a pad, and a pen in his small backpack. He set them beside his bed and sat on his chair. For the first time since this whole affair started, he was willingly choosing to go back to Zycodia. But not just right away. He had to wait for the right time.

After supper, he took a bath and pretended to get ready for bed. Instead, he stayed in bed fully dressed until he was sure everyone had gone to sleep. When he was certain that no one was awake, he repositioned his bed and then traveled to the other world.

— Chapter 31 —

To Search Again

Axel landed in front of the queen's chamber. "Ouch," he cried. "I really hate these landings." Axel knocked on the door.

The queen opened and said, "Axel, hi, come in."

Axel bowed and entered Queen Elyjanah's chambers.

She pressed a button on what Axel thought was an intercom. "So, Axel, what have you discovered?"

"I have an idea of where to look for the celestial gem of the Taurus tribe. I was helping my dad with his work, and the thought came to me."

"Really?" she exclaimed. "Then go on to the sacred room. I believe that, this time, your search will be successful."

Axel headed to the room and got the belt. When he stepped out, Ujin was waiting in the queen's chambers. The queen was speaking to him. "Axel came earlier than we expected. He said he has an idea of how to find the celestial gem. Take him to Chief Tiroh right away, please."

"Yes, your majesty." He bowed and led Axel down to the fifth level again. They went through the door and swiftly traveled to the land of the Tauruses. Upon reaching the Chief's home, Ujin parked in front of the massive house and knocked on the door. The new butler, Thom, greeted them again and led them in. "I'll let the chief know you are here."

Amora appeared in the hallway. "Wow, you're back right away. Miss me already?"

Thom came back and led them to Chief Tiroh's study. This time, he was sitting behind his desk. He looked up and said, "Well, well, back so soon?"

"Yes, sir. I think I have an idea where to look for... *it*." Axel did not say 'celestial gem' because Thom was lingering in the room.

"Okay. Amora can go with you again. Thom, call her?"

"She was just here, sir." Thom said, and they all looked behind him, but Amora was not there.

In a flash, Amora appeared. "I'm here!" She was all dressed up and ready to go.

Axel covered his mouth to suppress his giggling. He thought this would be another fun time with Amora.

She said excitedly, "Come on. Let's go."

"You have your communicator, so call if you need me," Ujin reminded Axel.

— CHAPTER 32 —

Saving Amora

Amora hopped onto her bright, shinny, pink bike and powered up the engine before Axel was able to settle into the seat. As the bike zoomed down the hill, Axel gripped the side handle of the front seat with all his strength.

"Stop! Amora, stop!" he yelled, as he struggled to lift his right leg up onto the bike.

"Why?"

"I'm not seated yet."

She stepped hard on the brakes at the bottom of the hill, throwing Axel off the bike.

"What are you doing down there?"

Axel responded annoyingly, You sped up before I could even sit on the bike. That's why I yelled for you to stop."

"Which I did, so?"

"So, I lost my grip and fell."

"Well, sorry. Hop on now."

"Fine." Axel stood up in pain and got on the bike.

"I assume you know where we should go."

"Not really."

Amora frowned. "I thought that's why you came back so soon."

"Yes, I have an idea of what to look for but not where to look for it. How about just driving through the streets again?"

"Fine." She powered her bike again and drove through the streets. They went around the rotunda of the shopping center and past the government buildings. There was a statue of a bull right in the center of the rotunda. Maybe it was intuition, or maybe it was imagination, but Axel found himself drawn to it. The huge statue depicted a proud, victorious bull that was standing on a pedestal.

"Amora, stop. Whose statue is that?"

"That's Bak, our hero from long ago. It was said that he alone defended our land from a whole army of invaders."

"How long has that statue been there?"

"It's been there since long before I was born, even long before my dad was born, too. We're talking about centuries here. No one bothers to go near it."

"Let's go closer."

"Why? Do you think that's where the gem is?"

"Maybe, no harm in looking, right?"

"Come on." Amora parked her bike at the side of the statue and jumped off. Again, this jerking motion made Axel bounce up and then fell back on the bike.

"Ouch, don't do that!" he exclaimed, looking irritated.

"Stop doing what? Why are you still sitting there?"

He gritted his teeth and got out.

They went closer to the statue. Axel looked at it and was awed by its enormity. He walked around the corded monument and remembered the riddle… *in plain sight, a stone untouched by time.* He leveled his eyes to the stones underneath the statue. He circled around again and then stopped on one side.

As he stepped backwards, with his hand on his chin, suddenly, his face lit up when a weird looking stone caught his eye. It rested behind the upward tilted heel of the statue's left hind foot. It was small, uniquely triangular, and seemed like it hadn't been touched or moved.

"Axel, Axel! Did you find something?"

He moved closer to the statue and carefully pulled out the stone. It was covered with dust and some spider webs. Amora's eyes widened with excitement. "Is that the one?"

"I don't know yet." he said, trying to brush away the dirt.

Amora handed him a bunch of tissues.

He continued to clean it and saw a glint of light behind the stone. "I think this is the one!"

"Now, what do we do?"

Axel hid the stone in his pant pocket and pressed the right button on his communicator. "Ujin, I think I found it."

"I'll be there right away."

Someone hit the back of Axel's head and knocked him down. As he was falling, he saw Thom, the butler, cover Amora's mouth and nose. She slumped into Thom's arms. Axel could hardly believe his eyes when Thom's face morphed into that of a cheetah with a foreboding Cheshire smile. He lifted Amora over his back and started to run.

Ujin arrived. "Axel, what happened?" He helped Axel to his feet.

"The butler! He kidnapped Amora! He knocked me down, made Amora faint, turned into a cheetah, and carried her that way!"

Ujin looked in the direction Axel was pointing.

"We must go catch him and save Amora!" Axel exclaimed, trying to follow after Thom. He took a few wobbly steps forward then started to fall.

Ujin caught him and led him to the jet. He made Axel sit and drink a bottle of water.

After a few minutes, Ujin asked, "How are you feeling now?"

"I'm getting better, thanks. Let's go catch him!" he exclaimed.

He took off running after Thom. He was faster than before, but no matter how hard he tried, he wasn't able to overtake Thom. Exhausted, Axel fell to the ground.

Seeing Axel's failed attempt, Ujin jumped inside his Swifty and rushed to follow them.

Axel tried to stand up again, but he realized that it was hopeless.

Ujin continued and got ahead of Thom. Putting some distance between them, Ujin got out of Swifty, pulled out a zapper, and fired at Thom's legs. Thom fell and dropped Amora.

Axel was able to regain his energy and ran towards Amora and Ujin. "I'm so sorry, I could not run as fast as I thought I could. I was useless."

Amora started to wake up and stood up with Ujin's help. She heard Axel and patted his shoulder. "No worries, thank you for trying."

Amora angrily transformed into a cow and started huffing and puffing as she pounced on the defeated cheetah.

Thom was still on the ground, unconscious, when few of Chief Tiroh's men arrived to pick him up.

"Let the Chief know we have Amora, and we will bring her home." Ujin said.

One of the men nodded as they placed Thom inside their vehicle.

Ujin signaled for Axel and Amora to enter their ride. Without anything else said, they headed to Chief Tiroh's house. The trip was fast and upon reaching the chief's house, they saw another person in the room dressed in white.

"This is Doctor Fitri. He is here to perform a checkup on Amora."

"I'm fine, dad. No need for a checkup."

"No whining," the Chief said in a commanding voice.

As Amora's examination was ending, they heard sirens, signaling the arrival of police officers. Chief Tiroh told Amora to open the door for them. One by one they marched inside, led by Deputy Higaro. Two police officers dragged Thom inside.

"Why did you kidnap my daughter?" the fuming chief commanded.

Thom was so scared to answer the chief. He was afraid that telling the truth would mean a death punishment from Sevion and Dulli.

"Higaro, take this scumbag and lock him in the dungeon."

"Uh, yes sir, but we have no dungeon."

"You know what I mean. Go before I smash his face."

"Yes, sir." Higaro ordered his men to take him.

The officers bowed as they moved out of the house with the prisoner. He was taken to the police station to be locked up in the prison cell.

When they were left alone, Tiroh turned to Ujin and Axel. "Thank you for saving my daughter."

Axel turned away, feeling embarrassed. "I'm sorry, sir. It was Ujin who saved Amora."

Chief Tiroh patted his back so hard that he almost gagged. "You tried, and that's important."

Axel retrieved the stone from his pocket and showed it to the chief. "Is the celestial gem inside this stone?"

Tiroh smiled. "Ah, yes. It is."

"The queen will tell you what to do," Ujin said. "We better head back to the castle."

Axel thanked the chief, and they said their goodbyes.

Amora walked them to the front door. She gave Axel a kiss on the cheek. "Thanks for trying to save me."

— CHAPTER 33 —

Second Bonding

Ujin and Axel returned to the castle, where the queen was eagerly waiting for them. "Congratulations, Axel. You saved Amora and found the celestial gem of the Tauruses. Show it to me."

Axel proudly pulled the stone from his pocket and handed it to the queen. The satisfaction of finding this second gem gave him a sense of accomplishment and pride.

"What does the rest of the riddle say?"

He recited the riddle, "In plain sight, a stone untouched by time—that I figured out, but the next part—embrace its beauty to own the might of nine. What does it mean?"

Queen Elyjanah explained. "The Tauruses are known for their incredible strength. If you bond with this gem, you could acquire great strength of nine men, just like you acquired the speed of the Cancers. Let's go to the sacred room now." The queen turned and walked towards the sanctuary, and Axel followed her.

"Now, remove the sash from your waist. Step up close to the pedestal and put the gem close to your heart. The orb will do the rest." With that said, the queen stepped out of the chamber.

Axel did as he was told. He placed the stone on his chest close to his heart. When it touched his body, the dirty covering began to crumble and slowly a glow, which was energy, emanated, exposing the shiny gem. This put him into a trance and lifted his body into the air. Slowly, the glow wrapped around his chest eventually covered his entire body. Unconsciously, Axel squirmed trying to free himself from the enclosure and heat, but no matter how hard he struggled, he couldn't escape.

Queen Elyjanah's words kept ringing in his mind. *"Don't fight the process. No matter how painful it may be, stay still, and you will be alright."* Like an automatic response, his body stopped moving. For several minutes, he was suspended in midair until the energy gradually flowed down to the belt, where it settled on the gem's symbol. Upon contact, Axel slowly descended to the ground before regaining consciousness.

He tried to regain his balance as he struggled to walk towards the door, where he turned the knob and exited.

The queen asked, "Well, Axel how do you feel?"

"Not sure yet. I bonded with the gem. I felt the energy flowing through my veins." Axel looked at the belt and felt the imbedded celestial gem. It was roundish and seemed to have two horns on top.

"Yes, that's right. Now that you have completed the task, return the belt. I'm sure it is time for you to go home."

He returned to the sacred room, and as he unfastened the belt, it again floated back onto the pedestal. Axel marveled every time he witnessed this phenomenon.

He rejoined Queen Elyjanah and Ujin in the hall.

"Would you like something to eat, Axel? You must be hungry."

"Yes, but I'm also tired. I just wanna go home." He was about to create the portal when he remembered the question he wanted to ask Queen Elyjanah. "Will I be able to use these powers on Earth?"

"Not now, but don't be disheartened. In the future, you may be able to tap into those powers in your homeland. Goodbye Axel, until next time. We shall await your return."

With the movement of his hand, Axel created the portal, said goodbye and then entered the void.

— CHAPTER 34 —

Back to School

Several weeks passed, and finals exams were approaching fast. Axel kept busy finishing essays and projects, as well as reviewing for the tests. He and Rena studied and took the exams together. They had become an item at school, and other kids called them the brainiac pair.

On their last day, Axel was working in the literary club room when Rena entered and joyfully cried out, "Finally, tests are over. We can now enjoy our summer vacation."

"You said it," Axel answered. "I'm just cleaning up the room. I'll be done in a few. Do you want to wait for me?"

"Of course. In fact, I'll help you."

Rena put some books back on the shelves while Axel cleaned the floor and then the tables. He also organized the files inside the cabinet drawers.

The club president came in and thanked them both for their hard work. He reminded Axel of the scheduled meeting at a restaurant, sort of a final get together. They all left the room, and the club president locked the door.

Axel and Rena walked home together.

"Axel, what will you be doing this summer?"

"I don't know, maybe work on cars with my dad. How about you?"

"Well, I'll be helping out with the Fourth of July parade. Speaking of which, can you come help with it too?"

"Sure, why not. Let me know when," Axel answered, as they got to Rena's house.

"Wanna come in?" she asked.

"Maybe next time. I promised my mom I would clean the backyard as soon as school ended."

"Great. I'll call you when we start working on the float, booths, or any of the tasks we are given."

"Bye. See you soon." With that, Axel headed home.

No one else was in the house. He put down his backpack and everything else he had brought home from school. Axel grabbed something to eat from the fridge. After he heated the food, he went over to the couch and turned on the tv. Flipping through the channels, only an animal show sparked his interest.

It didn't take long for him to get bored, so after he finished his meal, he went to the backyard to start cleaning. He was looking for the broom when he was startled by someone moving behind him. When he turned around, he was surprised to see Ujin, disguised as an old man.

"Hi, Axel, how are you?" he said with a smile.

"I'm fine. My hand is not hurting. Why are you here?" Axel responded with an irritated look.

"Goodness, is that any way to greet a friend?"

"I'm sorry, with exams and everything else, can't I take a break?"

"Fair enough. I'm here at the queen's orders. Being bonded with the celestial gem of the Taurus is not enough to wield power. You need to be able to control it. Otherwise, you could cause great destruction."

"And you tell me this after I get the celestial gem? How am I supposed to learn how to control it?"

"You need to return to Zycodia and train with the Libra monks."

"The who?"

"The monks from the Libra tribe. We can go there now, if you are ready."

"No, I'm not. My mom needs me to finish cleaning this backyard. I promised, so how about if I go tonight when everyone is asleep?"

"Fine. I'll see you later then." Ujin gave in and disappeared.

"I have to learn how he does that," Axel muttered to himself.

Because Axel was distracted thinking about what Ujin had said, he took much longer to clean the yard than he expected. His experiences in Zycodia were very distracting. Now, he'd heard his sisters talk about astrology and the zodiac signs, but he still wondered what the members of the Libra tribe could possibly shape-shift into… He shook his head to clear his mind and redoubled his effort to finish the task at hand.

— CHAPTER 35 —

Master Soli

Axel waited for everyone in his family to fall asleep before he got ready to travel. Knowing he was to undergo some sort of training, this time, he stuffed more snacks in his backpack. He made a final sweep of the bedrooms and saw everyone nicely tucked away in bed.

Inserting the ring on his finger and shouldering his backpack, he took a deep breath. He placed his hand on the tapestry, saying to himself, *"I don't think I'll ever get used to this travel."* He did not like going through the tunnel, but most of all, he hated the landings. No matter how he tried to prepare for his entrance to that world, the where and how were never the same. On the other hand, what he was always able to anticipate was the pain with every exit. This time, he landed headfirst on the floor. "Ouch. I really, really…"

Before he finished his sentence, Ujin greeted him with a smile. "Welcome back, Axel."

"How did you know I'd be here now?" Axel made sure he'd regained his balance before he sat up.

Ujin took his hand and helped him to his feet. "The queen told me, of course."

Axel nodded, "Why did I even ask? So, what do we do now?"

"I'll take you to the Libra monks, where you'll be trained by Master Soli."

Axel looked away, feeling somber. "I know I failed miserably in rescuing Amora; it was embarrassing. So, I suppose it is necessary for me to get more training." Suddenly, his face lit up. "Wait a minute, Ujin, what about the belt? Queen Elyjanah said that I should always wear the belt when I am here."

"Not this time. You will have to undergo training without the belt. Let's go."

When they reached the fifth level, Ujin opened the door to the room that Axel assumed led to Libra's territory. The room was quite empty, with just a few chairs. There were no decorations or statues, but there was a picture of a temple and some books on a shelf. Ujin's trusty jet was parked outside the exit door. It was as swift as ever, and in no time, they sped out of the tunnel. He wondered again what creatures the Libra people would be.

As the jet slowed down, three landing gears were deployed and touched the ground. Ujin drove the jet like a car through a single lane in a vast, open field. The view was miles and miles of wide empty space as far as the eye could see.

"There's nothing here. How far do we still have to go? And why did you not just fly over this place instead of driving through the road?"

"Not that far. The monks' compound is at the end of this road. It stretches through hills for several miles. I had to drive because the monks do not like jets flying over their place. They said it's too noisy and loud for them."

As they approached their destination, Axel saw an area enclosed by a tall fence. Ujin halted in front of the huge gate. A man wearing monk clothes similar to those of Earth opened the gate wide enough for Ujin to drive in. He parked his jet in front of a white building that looked like a temple from Earth's Middle Ages. The building's façade was lined with sculptured columns and several steps led to the wooden front door.

A younger-looking man also dressed like a monk ushered them up the stairs and into the temple. The place was so quiet that only their footsteps were audible. Not only was the temple quiet, but it was also eerily dim. They entered a room that was illuminated by several candles lined up close to the wall. The young man bowed to them and left the room.

After several minutes, a short and stocky elderly man with a balding head entered the room. He was wearing a long, dark brown, hooded robe with a cord tied around his waist. A pendant shaped like a scale hung from the chain around his neck. He also wore pointed sandals that looked like small boats.

With a big smile on his face, he trotted towards Ujin and Axel. "Hello, Ujin. Good to see you again." It was Master Soli, and he extended his hand to greet Ujin and his companion as well. "You are Axel, I presume."

"Yes," he answered shyly with a bow, as he was unsure of how to interact with the monk.

"Come, come. Let's have something to drink." He led the way to a dining area. Another monk served them drinks. "This is juice from our fruit trees, similar to what you call a coconut."

Ujin said, "Thank you, Master Soli, for agreeing to this request." Ujin slapped Axel's back, making Axel almost spit out his drink. "Axel, here, needs a lot of training to control his energy. Honestly, he hardly has control of anything."

"I do, too!" Axel complained.

"Oh, you think you do?" retorted the Master.

"I, um, think so."

Ujin asked, "How long do you think this training can take?"

"Depends on Axel and how determined he can be." Master Soli frowned. "Are you aware that our treasure was stolen?"

"Yes, the queen and I know it. That is why it is urgent that you train Axel. He needs to retrieve the treasure to be able to continue his quest, his destiny."

"Wait a minute," interrupted Axel. "What happened to your treasure?"

Master Soli explained, "Some months ago, our celestial gem was stolen. We have been open to everyone, so maybe it's our fault that our guard was down. We never imagined anyone would defile our temple and steal our treasure." He looked sad for a moment. "I know who stole it… he was one of my best students, but I do not know why he took it or where he went."

"Why did you not take it back?"

"The number of students requesting training has recently doubled, so much of my time and energy has been dedicated to extending our facilities and caring for our students. I have every intention of retrieving our treasure, of course, when the time is right."

"Queen Elyjanah is hoping Axel will be ready soon, I mean, to help find your gem." Ujin stood up and turned to Axel. "I will now have to leave you in Master Soli's excellent care. I will come back when it is time for you to go home."

Extending his hand to Master Soli, he bowed and said, "Thank you."

— CHAPTER 36 —

The Training Begins

Master Soli took Axel to an empty room at the end of the hallway. It was dimly lit by round sconces attached to the walls. Upon entering the room, he stopped to face Axel and, with a serious face, gave the new trainee a stern warning.

"Axel, training will be rigid, very hard. There will be no rest, no slacking, no mercy, you hear? I will teach you to balance your mind and body, control and focus your energy. You will undergo tests of endurance, stamina, and determination. When I'm done with you, you will be able to harness incredible strength and power—but enough said, let's start."

Master Soli walked towards the side wall and pressed one of the wooden panels that revealed a closet door. He took out a foot-long cone that was about six inches in diameter at the base and three inches at the top.

"Axel. Place your right foot on top of the cone. Then lift your body to stand on it. Keep your left leg close and bend it, so you stay balanced. Raise your left and right arms up to form a straight, horizontal line. Keep this position until the hand on the timer points down then get down and switch to your left leg until the hand on the timer points upward. You will repeat this task until I tell you to stop."

"What? I can't do that!" Axel protested. "I didn't sign up for this kind of torture."

Master Soli smacked Axel's head and angrily yelled, "Are you a wimp?"

"No, I'm not, but this is really too hard for me." In that instant, Axel froze, watching his teacher transform into a huge mass that slowly took the shape of an owl, a very large owl.

It bent over him with its big, dark eyes glaring angrily at him. In a deep scary voice, it uttered, "no mercy."

Axel fell on his backside. "Okay, okay! I'm going." He scrambled to get on the cone but quickly fell. He got up and fell on the floor again.

"Keep your body and right leg straight and bend the left one. If your posture is crooked, you will surely fall. Raise your arms to be level with your shoulders. Use your mind to balance your body. Lower your arms when you feel you are in perfect vertical alignment."

Axel followed Master Soli's instructions. He lifted himself up but fell again. This went on for so long that Axel lost count of how many times he tried to balance on the cone.

When he finally succeeded in balancing on top of the cone, Master Soli reverted to his humanoid form. He then turned on something that looked like a clock but had no numbers, just lines. "This is a timer and I've set it to begin. If you fall the timer will reset to begin again."

"What!?" Axel exclaimed and fell.

"Get up and start over," he said and reset the time.

When Axel was able to balance for a few minutes, Master Soli went to the other side of the wall, got a pillow, and plopped it on the floor. He sat down in a lotus position and closed his eyes. He also placed an hourglass next to him.

As upset as Axel was, he had no choice other than to obey the master. He was so tired, and after thirty minutes, he was ready to get down. He was about to set a foot down when Master Soli, opening one eye shaking his head, said, "Nuh, uh uh."

Axel growled but relented. Luckily, he was able to regain his balance and made it through the rest of the hour.

When the last grain of this hour glass dropped, an alarm rang…marking the end of this training, which to Axel lasted forever. Now, all Axel wanted to do was go home and sleep.

— CHAPTER 37 —

At The River

After two grueling hours on the cone, Axel felt exhausted and hungry. At the sound of the alarm, he descended from the cone, dropped on his knees, and let his body collapse.

Master Soli stood up and signaled Axel to follow him. Axel wobbled toward the door and picked up his backpack. He opened a snack bar then took a sip from his water bottle.

"Master Soli, wait... wait," he called, trying to catch up.

The master continued walking as though he heard nothing. They headed toward the front door. Coming from inside the dark temple, Axel rubbed his eyes to adjust to the brightness outside. Breathing the fresh air felt so good that for a few moments he forgot his hunger.

He tried to keep up with the master. "So, Master Soli, is my training done?"

Master Soli turned to face him. "I told you, no mercy. Hurry up, slowpoke."

"Yeah, yeah." Axel stuck out his tongue and made faces behind the master who said, "I saw that. Demerits for you."

"What do you mean?"

"You'll find out."

"So where are we going now?"

"Will you stop asking questions? You are giving me a headache."

The topographic view of the monastery's land stretched for miles from the mountainside, through hills, and down to the lowlands. The panoramic view of the trees, shrubs, flowers, and lush grass covering the ground like carpet was breathtaking.

Master Soli and Axel continued walking until they reached a river that passed through the monastery's compound. The water was just about five feet deep, but it was flowing at a fast speed downhill. They climbed to the next hill, where Axel saw two poles on opposite sides of the stream. Each pole had supported a platform and had a ladder leading up its side. A sturdy rope stretched above the river, connecting the two structures.

Master Soli pointed at the poles. "Those, my dear boy, are called Falcon's Perches."

"Let me guess," Axel scoffed. "I gotta hang on the rope like a monkey and cross that river, right?"

"Um, good guess, but not the right one." Master Soli smiled. "You have to climb up to the pole and walk on the rope to cross the river."

"Are you serious? I could hardly balance myself on that cone, and my legs are still shaking."

"Wah, wah, wah, always complaining." Master Soli turned around and headed toward a separate post nearby. On top of this post was a wheel from which long poles hung arranged in a circle.

Master Soli grabbed one of these poles and gave it to Axel. "Here, use this to balance yourself as you walk on the rope."

Axel took it and was surprised by how light it was. "I thought the pole would be heavy."

"Nope. These poles are made from trees much like bamboo trees in your world."

Standing in front of the ladder, he did not want to move and wondered again why he had to be the one to do this.

"Because you are a very important person, Chosen One," Master Soli retorted with a huge grin on his face.

Axel groaned as he realized that he had said his thoughts aloud.

"Get going, you are wasting my time." Master Soli started poking Axel's behind again and again until he stepped onto the ladder.

"Stop that now," Axel protested. Reaching the top of the ladder, he balanced himself on the landing, which just had enough space for both his feet. Positioning the pole horizontally close to his waist, he adjusted and balanced it with both hands.

Master Soli shouted to him, "Be careful not to fall. If you do, I may not be able to save you from the flowing river."

"Thanks a lot," Axel yelled with a smirk on his face.

Reluctantly, he stepped on the rope with his right foot. Slowly, he put his left foot forward while stabilizing his balance.

He was about ten steps away from where he started when he heard Master Soli shouting, "Remember not to fall."

Hearing this warning, Axel began to lose his concentration. He started swaying from side to side trying to regain his balance. His left foot slipped from the rope, and he tumbled towards the water, yelling for help. "Master Soli, I can't swim!"

Axel plunged into the river which rapidly carried him downstream. He kept yelling for help, but Master Soli or any other monk was nowhere in sight. When he was dropped from a steep incline in the river, the water slowed down to a steady flow. He rolled down until he hit something that felt like wood. He held on to it and opened his eyes. It was a bamboo pole that stopped him from flowing any farther. He looked around and then saw Master Soli on the left side of the river and another monk on the other side. They were holding the pole and laughing their hearts out. *Oh, for crying out loud, laugh more, would you?* he thought bitterly, as he tried to pull himself out of the water.

Axel was soaked to the bone, as he laid on the grass taking great heaving breaths. His ears were ringing. Master Soli approached him and started talking, but Axel's eyes began to blur, and his world darkened, as he slipped out of consciousness, unaware of what Master Soli was trying to say.

Axel was awakened by a humming sound. He opened his eyes to see where he was, and, to his surprise, he was in the same room where he stood on the cone for two hours. He was on the floor with his head on a pillow. He tried as hard as he could to remember what happened to him, but his memory started only from the time he climbed out of the river. He wondered how he got to the temple. He had no recollection at all.

He moved his body and sat up. He felt okay, except for his hand that was starting to throb. He looked at it and saw a flicker of light. He realized he had been in Zycodia for almost a day. This had never happened since he started coming to this world.

Master Soli entered the room and noticed Axel's hand. "Ah, so your stay is almost over."

"Is that why my hand is glowing?"

"Yes, yes, better hurry. As soon as the glow stops, you won't be able to go home."

"Whoa. Master Soli, thanks for the training."

Axel created the portal and, in a flash, was sucked into the tunnel and out of the tapestry. He fell straight on his bed. He had never felt happier to lay down and sleep.

— Chapter 38 —

Fourth of July Preparations

A warm sunrise that promised a bright day woke Axel up after a very long sleep. He still felt achy, but with a few stretches of his arms and legs, he seemed normal again. He had no plans other than relaxing. His stomach was growling, as he headed to the bathroom to take a bath before going to the kitchen.

Sarah saw him get out of the bathroom. Wearing her favorite pink colored apron with a fruit design and her name stitched above it, she cheerfully greeted Axel. "There you are. You woke up so late! It'll be almost time for lunch."

He followed his mom to the kitchen and found that he was the last one at the dining table. "Is there still some breakfast left, mom? I'm so hungry, I could probably eat three platefuls."

"I'm preparing to cook lunch, but there are some leftover pancakes and fried bacon from breakfast. I can cook some eggs for you. How do you want them?"

"Scrambled, please."

"Just wait a few minutes. Check the oven to see if there are still bread rolls. After this breakfast meal, you may not have any room for lunch."

"That's okay." Axel placed the pancakes and bacon on a plate. He took the bread rolls, which were still warm.

Sarah placed the cooked scrambled eggs on his plate.

"Thanks, mom" he said, as he started to eat.

Sleeping was good, and breakfast was great. Axel was content for now. He was cleaning the table when they heard a knock on the door. Axel went to see who it was. To his delight, it was Rena.

"Hi Axel. July fourth is the day after tomorrow. The booths must be completed today. You said you'd help, remember? Are you free now?"

"Yeah, sure. Let me just quickly change, and I can go with you. Would you like to wait for me, or do you just want to meet there?"

"I'll wait," she answered.

"Okay, so come in."

As soon as Axel got dressed, they headed toward the village circle. They decided to take the back road shortcut to the entrance.

The place was already bustling with men putting up booths and pushing crates of beer and soda. Rena and Axel saw Anita, who was the program coordinator. She was so glad to see two more volunteers.

"What would you like us to do, Anita?" Rena inquired.

"The streamers need to be put up. You can hang the streamers from one booth to another going around the circle. There's a ladder in my truck that you can use. The streamers are also there. We are grilling hot dogs and sandwiches for lunch, so come back here when you get hungry, okay?"

Axel and Rena set out to carry out their task by heading to the truck. Axel picked up the ladder while Rena dragged the streamers. They started with the booth that was closest to the entrance. As he positioned the ladder near the edge of the post, Rena unbundled the load and then handed him the end of the string. He stood in front of the ladder but hesitated to go up.

At first, Rena waited, but after a few minutes, she seemed confused. "Hey, Axel, we can't get this done unless you climb up and start hanging."

Flashes of his training with Master Soli had stunned Axel into a trance, and memories of his experiences flooded in his mind. He did not even hear what Rena said.

"Earth to Axel!" Rena said, tugging his arm. "What happened to you? You were just standing there."

Axel took a deep breath and stepped onto the ladder. "Oh nothing, I just remembered something." He continued to climb and when he reached the highest step, he hung the end of the streamer on top of the booth post. After that first hold up, they gained momentum going from booth to booth. There were no other hitches until they went full circle to the last post.

An hour past noon, they were done. They returned the ladder to Anita's truck and joined the other volunteers for lunch. They rested a bit before making posters and signs for the rest of the afternoon.

Going home, on the way to Rena's house, Axel had a thought. "Rena, you're an excellent swimmer. Can I ask you a favor?"

"Yeah, sure. What is it?"

"Can you teach me how to swim?"

"Really? It never occurred to me that you didn't know how to swim."

"My mom tried to teach me when I was younger, but then she became so busy with the bakery, you know."

"It's not that hard, sure, I can teach you. It's summer, perfect time to go swimming anyway."

"Thanks, just let me know when you have the time." Upon reaching Rena's house, Axel said, "Bye, see you tomorrow at the fair."

Rena replied, "Well, it's I who need to thank you for helping with the fair preparations."

"No biggie, my pleasure." He waved goodbye and headed home.

— Chapter 39 —

After the Fair

The fourth of July fair went well. Despite the heat, everyone seemed to enjoy the festivities. As it had been a yearly tradition, Sarah baked pies and cookies to sell. Axel helped set up the booth for his mom and dad, but he spent most of the day with Rena and, of course, Shushu. To Sarah's delight, Rena volunteered to help sell their pies and cookies. During breaks, they played some games and even went on rides.

The plaza got crowded toward lunchtime and through the afternoon. Food and drinks were continuously sold in the marketplace close to their booth. Guests were still coming even when the darkness of the night started creeping in. As the sun faded away, strings of lightbulbs turned on, illuminating the entire area. Everyone around the fountain cheered as the different colored rays danced through the water flow.

The fireworks that brightened up the skies flashed along to the tempo of patriotic songs, while onlookers were awed by the spectacle. Most of the guests proceeded to the dance area, but Axel and Rena decided to go home with their families. After changing into his pajamas, he fell asleep as soon as his head touched the pillow.

It was around three-thirty in the morning when Axel was awakened by the pain in his hand. He looked at it, hoping that it was just a dream, but to his dismay, a flicker of light flashed in his eyes. He got up, annoyed, and sat on his bed to collect his thoughts. He tried to rub his palm to see if the pain would go away. Of course, it didn't.

Slowly, he got out of bed and staggered to the closet to get his backpack. He crept silently to the kitchen to gather some snacks for the trip. He also brought a small flashlight, a pen, his journal, and the watch he got for his birthday.

Before he left, he checked each room to see if everyone was asleep, then he returned to his bedroom, wrapped the sash around his waist, and put the ring on his finger. With a deep sigh, he placed his hand at the center of the tapestry.

The portal appeared, and he was whirled away at an incredible speed. He hated this transport. It always made him feel nauseous. After travelling a few times through this tunnel, he discovered the way to survive this perilous journey was to close his eyes until he landed somewhere, which was never the same place. At the touchdown, he gazed at an open field. "Geez, now where am I?"

The morning sun was just starting to rise and, not knowing where he landed, Axel started to panic. He looked around and saw the goat, Rolin. "Welcome back, Axel. How are you? I have been monitoring your progress, and I am very pleased".

"Why are you here?" Axel asked.

"Ujin is busy with tasks of vital importance for Her Majesty. Now, do you remember what I spoke of with Ujin when we first met—that I promised Ujin my assistance if he should need it? I must aid you through this enormous destiny of yours. I am a teacher and a counselor, and I know you feel this destiny is an unsurmountable burden. There will be defeats and failures along the way, but cheer up. I believe you are a brave young man who can overcome the obstacles that come your way." Done with his pep talk, Rolin started walking. "Come on, Axel, let's get you going to see Master Soli."

Axel quietly followed Rolin. Preoccupied with Rolin's words, he was oblivious to the unending road they seemed to tread. Upon reaching a familiar structure up a hill, the temple of the Libras, he was shaken back to reality when Rolin declared, "We are here."

The walk to the temple took about thirty minutes, based on his watch. He was surprised that the gate was not locked, just closed. When they reached the temple, Rolin tried to open the front door. It was locked. He quietly tapped the door, trying not to cause a ruckus.

One of the monks named Lunka opened the door and was surprised not to see Ujin with Axel. "Oh, hi, Sir Rolin. You're here so early." He smiled at Axel. "I'll tell Master Soli you are here." He went back inside while Axel drank his juice.

Master Soli stepped out in no time. "Hi, Professor Rolin."

"Hi, Master Soli. Ujin is busy now, so I came to have a chat with Axel and accompany him to your temple. For now, I bid you farewell, as I know he is in excellent hands." With that, Rolin bowed, turned, and walked away.

"Axel, I didn't expect you to come back so soon."

"I had no choice, Master Soli." Axel pointed to his hand. "So, here I am."

"Come in and have some warm food."

Axel followed Master Soli inside. Lunka was already in the dining area preparing a meal composed of bread, eggs, and fruits. He offered Axel a juice bottle, but he asked for water instead.

After eating, Axel just relaxed and looked around while waiting for the monks to complete their morning prayers. Because the temple was on top of a hill, he could see the river that flowed from the mountain and some parked vehicles next to another building located on the low flatland about a quarter mile away.

Axel was still enjoying the view and fresh air when Master Soli came out and signaled for him to come in. They went straight to the training room, and Master Soli took out the cone again.

Axel exclaimed, "No, not that again!"

"Yes, this again," answered Master Soli. "And no mercy. Up you go. Do the same thing you did before, but four repetitions this time."

"What?" Axel's protest fell on deaf ears.

Master Soli poked Axel's behind, forcing him to get up on the cone. He did as he was told, and the task was a bit easier than before. So, he positioned himself on top of the cone and grinned as if to show his master that this wasn't a big deal anymore.

Master Soli left the room. Another monk stayed to watch over Axel. After an hour, Axel's leg started to feel numb from standing. He wanted to get down or even to bend his knees, but if he did, Master Soli reminded him that his two hours would restart. Feeling defeated and upset, he endured the torture by closing his eyes and daydreamed about Rena, his bed, and all the other comforting memories from his home world.

After the grueling four hours, Master Soli took Axel back to the river where the poles were located. He was about to get up when Master Soli gave him different instructions. This time, instead of balancing on top, he had to cross the river by hanging from the rope. Thinking that this would prove to be an easier task, he confidently climbed up the ladder and sat on the platform. Slowly, he gripped the rope with his hands, lowered himself, and started to move forward—left hand then right—trying to reach the other side of the river.

Realizing that he overestimated his strength when his grip started to slip, he raised his arm to hug the rope. He felt too numb to move anymore.

"Get going," Master Soli yelled to him.

After a few moments of rest, Axel lowered himself and started to move on. To his dismay, he slipped and fell into the river… *again*. The water flow carried him downward until he was blocked by the bamboo pole held by Lunka and another monk.

They were laughing at him louder than they had the first time he fell. Axel crawled out of the river and laid on the grass. Master Soli said, "Axel, let's go back to the temple, and we can give you some clothes to change into."

On their walk back, he saw kids his age doing some exercises near the other building. "Are those your students?"

"Yes, they are. Everyone is doing well, too."

"Are they also forced to do the training?"

"Oh no. Their parents enroll them, and I accept them if and only if they are one hundred percent sure they want to be here."

When they got back to the temple, Axel was given a new set of clothes, monk clothes.

"Don't you have clothes like mine?"

Master Soli ignored his question. "We'll just hang your clothes to dry. Now go change. Then you start on your next challenge, which is running!"

He took off his wet clothes and put on the ones given to him. He joined Master Soli outside the temple. "How can I even run with these clothes?" he asked with a frown.

"Now, now. Don't complain. If I can run in these clothes, so can you. You'll be going around the entire compound."

They walked towards the place where some vehicles were parked. Master Soli rode a bike and then he said to Axel, "Start running, go that way." He pointed to the open grounds.

"Why are you on the bike? I thought you could run in these clothes."

Master Soli grinned. "Because you'll have to catch up with me. I ride, you run. Let's go."

Axel started to run. At first, he was running side by side with Master Soli's bike. When the flat land ended and they got to hilly areas, Axel started to lag.

Because he did not have the belt for this training, no matter how fast he ran, Master Soli made his bike go even faster. They went around the entire compound until Axel collapsed and had no more energy to go any farther. Master Soli stopped his bike and helped Axel into the back seat of the vehicle. They headed back to the temple.

Surprisingly, Axel was given a generous lunch. It was a late meal, and he was given food he didn't recognize, but whatever it was, he did not complain. He just ate it all. His clothes were returned to him, and he was allowed to rest for about two hours; but as exhausted as he was, he was unable to sleep. He just laid on the floor and closed his eyes, again daydreaming of being on his bed or slouching on the couch watching TV.

Master Soli shook him to get up. It was time for the next training challenge. They walked out to the area where Axel saw students were training. There was something he failed to notice before… actually, two somethings. Axel wondered, *now what could those things be?*

— Chapter 40 —

More Training

As they came closer to the objects, Axel realized they looked like mechanical robots. Each had two padded, arm-like extensions, left and right. The head on top had two big, round, black eyes, a small, round, silver nose, and a rectangular opening for a mouth. Standing almost as tall as Axel and with two legs and feet that were clumped to a base, the pair looked weird and scary. That's when Axel noticed the two-foot grill fence surrounding the robots. *Why would they put robots in an enclosure? It's not like they can run away,* Axel thought with a smile.

"What are you smiling about?" Master Soli asked.

"Nothing."

"Huh, I don't think you'll be smiling when you face Klaper."

Axel started to chuckle. "So, these things have names? Which one is Klaper?"

"This is not just a thing. This is your trainer now." He unlocked the small gate in the fence. "Now get in." Master Soli ordered.

"There's hardly any room in there. What am I supposed to do with them?"

"You really do whine a lot. When Klaper starts moving, all you need to do is to block the arms, like this." Master Soli demonstrated what to do.

"That seems easy enough, I think."

"Very well, then, get inside."

Axel obeyed. Master Soli closed the gate and pressed a button on what looked like a remote control. Klaper started to turn and the left arm of the one on his right hit Axel, who wasn't paying enough attention.

"Ouch," he cried.

"Watch out, be alert," the master warned as the other robot shifted direction and hit Axel with its right arm.

"Ouch!" he cried again, bending low to avoid another strike.

"I told you to be alert. Watch Klaper's movement and start blocking the arms. Avoiding them like that will not work because Klaper cannot be fooled so easily."

With that said, Klaper's arm movements to up and down, pounding hard on Axel's back. Before Klaper could hit Axel again, he crawled through the small space between Klaper and the fence to reach the robot's backside. He hurriedly stood up before it was able to turn toward him.

When the robot faced Axel, it repositioned its arms to extend sideways again and started hitting its target, Axel's body. Instinctively, Axel blocked the punch. Klaper shifted to the other arm and, again, Axel was able to counter the attack.

"Huh, think I can't do this, huh?" He proudly looked at Master Soli, who just pointed at Klaper.

At that moment, before Axel was able to react, Klaper's arm hit the back of his shoulder, and he fell down. Realizing his error, he crawled to the other side and immediately stood up to get ready for any punch attack. He learned his lesson and started to get into the rhythm of the robots' movements until he was able to block each punch thrown at him.

After Axel successfully blocked the robot's arms several times, they eventually slowed down. The mechanical rustling sound ebbed to total silence. He stood in place ready for more action in case it started moving again.

"Ahhh. Good job. Good job." Master Soli gleefully opened the gate to let Axel out.

Axel wiped his sweaty forehead. "Phew. I thought it would never end. That was brutal."

"I knew you could do it. Come, let's sit down, so you can rest until your next task."

They walked toward the table and benches that were located near the students doing some exercises. Lunka brought two cups and a pitcher of juice. Axel was so thankful he drank it in one gulp and took second and third servings. Lunka also brought his clothes which he tried to put on behind a bush.

"Master Soli, your students, how long do they have to train?"

Like Axel, he also drank some juice. "Well, it depends on how fast they learn—may take a year or more."

"Are they all from your community of Libras?

"Oh no, they are from different tribes… and if you're wondering if they can all shift shapes, not all of them can. Some training regiments may depend on what shape they can transform to. You will learn more the longer you stay with us."

"So, if their training may take a long time, then why do I have to undergo an accelerated training?"

The master chuckled. "Have you forgotten? You are the Chosen One. Challenges await you soon, maybe sooner than we know."

"Lucky me," Axel muttered sarcastically.

Master Soli whipped Axel's back. "Don't talk that way. You should be honored." He stood up and motioned for Axel to do the same. He shook his head in annoyance and started walking. "Kids, they do not know responsibility, honor, or self-sacrifice, huh."

"Now where are we going?"

The master ignored Axel's question and kept walking. He stopped in front of what looked like a shed and opened the door of a small, empty room. There were three small windows on each side of the shed and beneath them were six orb-like structures, three on each side wall.

"Let me guess. We have to do some sparring here, right?"

"You wish." He flipped a switch. Lights turned on, and a low-pitched sound started buzzing. Suddenly, the round structures on the wall projected horizontally one at a time. "Okay. What you have to do is to kick the extended horizontal poles one at a time with your feet. If you kick the pole correctly, the extension will recede inward. Do the same for each pole until you reach the other end and then return back to the door."

"What? How do I do that with all those things moving in and out?"

Master Soli sighed with exasperation again. "You are such a dope." He pressed a button on the wall, and the floor started to move forward. "This is the way to do it." He stepped on the moving ramp and kicked the first pole on the right side then the next pole that extended from the left side, continuing in a pattern until he reached the other side. He pressed the power button again, and the poles and floor stopped moving. "Did you watch carefully what I did?"

Axel nodded.

"Are you ready?" Master Soli asked.

Axel shook his head, but Master Soli grabbed his hair and used it to move Axel's head up and down. "Yes, you are."

Master Soli turned on the switch. The floor moved forward, and the horizontal poles extended one by one from the wall. It was nerve-wracking to pass through because it was either kick or be kicked.

Axel hesitated.

"Get going. We don't have all day."

Axel had no choice but to start kicking the circular ends of the poles. With the first kick, the pole receded to the wall. The next was also a hit, but as the third pole came closer to him, he missed the target. The pole hit him, and he tripped toward the fourth pole, which swept him off his feet and onto the floor. Afraid of being hit again, Axel crawled under the poles and out of the structure.

"I've had enough, Master Soli. I'm tired, and I wanna go home."

Master Soli prodded him towards the structure, but Axel refused to move. "Very well. You should have said so. I would have sent you home after the river fall." He said this smiling.

Axel grunted and created the portal. Without saying goodbye, he went through the tunnel and dropped on his bed.

― Chapter 41 ―

Final Test

For the next three weeks, despite his protests, Axel had to go to Zycodia almost every other day to continue his training. With every session, he grew stronger and faster. His fighting skills advanced, both defensively and offensively. He was able to run as fast as Master Soli's bike, stand on the cone for three hours each leg, and cross the river on the tightrope—over or under—without using a bamboo pole to balance. His biggest success came from beating the two exercise structures because even though he mastered the rhythmic pattern of the punches, Master Soli gradually increased the speed each time he returned.

On the twenty-fifth day of training, Ujin was waiting for him next to Master Soli. "Hello, Axel. Master Soli told me that you completed your training. It's now time for your final test."

"What final test? Were those torturous tasks not enough?"

Master Soli interjected, "See what I had to go through with this whiny brat?"

Ujin laughed. "I know what you mean." He turned to Axel. "Well, training is great, but applying it to a real situation is a different story. For this test, we need to go back to the castle." Ujin powered his jet and opened the roof. He looked at Master Soli and bowed. "Thank you for training this numbskull. We are extremely grateful."

Master Soli responded with a bow. "It is our honor, and if he passes his final test, maybe he'll help us retrieve our treasure. Isn't that right, Axel?"

"Of course, I will do my best." He bowed before he entered the jet. "Bye, Master Soli."

The ride to the castle was swift. They proceeded to the queen's chambers, where she was waiting for their arrival.

"Hello, Axel, how are you?" The queen signaled for Axel to sit on the couch.

"I'm tired and worried about the final test or training or whatever it is."

"Come, let's go to our sacred room."

They went inside and the belt floated off the pedestal to wrap around him. After it settled on his waist again, they stepped out, and she said, "Ujin will take you to the dueling chamber and explain what you need to do. Good luck."

He now bowed instinctively. "Thank you."

Ujin and Axel rode the elevator to the second level. They entered the armory, passed through the middle hallway, and entered an empty room.

"Here, you will face a formidable opponent: a huge ogre. The challenge is to defeat it. Use anything you can find inside to defend yourself. I will be outside this room waiting for you."

Axel frowned. "Wait a minute, can't I bring a weapon with me?"

Ujin shook his head then pressed a button on the wall. The room transformed from an empty, four-wall room to a forest.

"Whoa, how did that happen? Did we get transported outside?"

"Remember, our world is a magical place, so anything is possible. There will be things you can use as weapons. Use your resourcefulness. Most of all, you must depend on your strength and wit to defeat this ogre. Ready?"

"Not really," Axel said, pouting.

Ujin shook his head, stepped out, and closed the door. Suddenly, a huge, furry monster appeared in front of him. It had angry eyes that stared at him and a full set of pointed teeth that stuck out when its mouth was wide open. It was much bigger than Axel and had sharp claws.

The creature's thundering roar caused Axel to fall backwards. He scrambled back, got up, and ran away. With fear enveloping his body and his heart beating so fast, his mind couldn't focus on what to do. He instinctively hid behind a rock to catch his breath.

Calming his nerves helped recover his wits, but not long after, he felt the ground beneath him shake. He peeped around the side of the rock and saw the ogre coming closer to him. It was using its nose to sniff out its prey—Axel.

Axel panicked and ran farther away again. To his shock and dismay, the trees began to thin out. There was a clearing beyond the forest. He kept running, but the ogre was closing in on him. When he reached the clearing, the ogre was only ten feet behind him. Axel had nowhere to go. Changing his strategy, Axel decided to stop and, with his power of speed, ran around the ogre as fast as he could. The monster tried to follow Axel's movements. Around and around, it went until it slowed down, too dizzy to move, and collapsed.

All the running made Axel tired. He tried to rest while the ogre was down, but that didn't last long. Suddenly, a bright idea flashed in his mind, or so he hoped. With this idea, he felt a surge of energy flow back through his body, as he came up with a plan.

He decided to run back to the forest and hide behind a tree. The ogre followed him, and before it got too close, Axel picked up a big rock and threw it as hard as he could. The rock hit the ogre in the eye. Axel threw another rock, a bigger one with sharp edges. This time, it struck the ogre's head, making the monster lose its footing and fall backwards. Axel ran into the heart of the forest, seeking higher ground.

Hearing a grunt, Axel turned to look behind him and saw the ogre get up and start walking again. Spying his target, Axel ran to the back side of a wide tree, where he quickly climbed up, balanced his body on a branch, and stayed out of the ogre's line of sight. As soon as it walked past the tree, Axel leapt off the branch and jumped on the ogre's back, forcing it to fall on the ground, face down.

The ogre tried to get up, but Axel was ready and gave it a big kick on the head, making it fall again. This time, the ogre did not get up. Axel poked its head with a tree branch, but it still laid flat on the ground. Axel sat down, leaned on the nearby tree, and let out a big sigh of relief.

He was still resting when suddenly, with whirlwind effect, Axel felt like he was transported away from the forest.

He looked up and saw Ujin smiling at him.

Axel thought, *I never saw him smile like that.*

"Very impressive, Axel. Congratulations. You defeated the ogre," he said, as he helped Axel stand up. "Now let's go see the queen."

Axel followed Ujin to the elevator and up to the queen's chambers.

Queen Elyjanah greeted him with a big smile. "Great, Axel! You've completed your training. You can now go home and relax for a few days."

"Just a few days? How about several months? Or a year?"

She sat on the couch. "Sorry. It may just be a few days until you will have to return. You have a mission to fulfill."

"What kind of mission?

"I cannot tell you. For now, go home and get lots of rest. Goodbye, Axel. Be good."

Axel opened the portal, traveled back home, and landed on his very own bed.

— CHAPTER 42 —

Time for Swimming Lessons

After sleeping almost half a day, Axel got up and went to the kitchen to find something to eat. The microwave clock showed it was one-thirty in the afternoon. There was pizza in the freezer, which he put into the microwave oven to cook.

He got some juice and an apple from the refrigerator. When the trusty appliance buzzed, Axel used tongs to transfer the hot pizza to a plate. He carried his meal to the den and turned on the television. No one was home, so it was a peaceful, restful time.

As always, Axel was only interested in the Discovery channel. To his disappointment, the current show was just a re-run of an episode he watched a few months ago. After finishing his meal, he decided to visit Rena.

The weather was sunny and hot, but Axel did not mind the heat. He was just thankful he was home. Besides, he felt stronger and more agile. He flexed his arms—he almost felt like Superman. Pumped with energy, he jogged the rest of the way to Rena's house.

Unsure if she was home, he knocked on the door, and to his surprise, Rena was there.

"Hi, Axel. How've you been? Come inside."

He stepped in and went to the living room couch, as if this was already his home.

Rena asked, "Care for a drink?"

"No thanks. I'm good. I was just... umm... wondering when we can go swimming."

"Oh, how about tomorrow morning, Saturday?"

"Cool. I'll ask my mom to drive us to the pool," Axel responded excitedly.

"How would you like to play a video game now?"

"Sure, it's been a long time since I played any game."

"Great." Rena started the game, and they played for two hours until Axel remembered the note his mom tacked on the refrigerator with a magnet.

"Oh no, I just remembered. My mom asked me to mow the lawn, so I gotta go." He stood up and returned the controller to the table. "What time tomorrow?"

"Nine-ish," Rena answered as she opened the door.

"Awesome, thanks."

It took Axel an hour to mow the lawn. Sarah had to work a little longer in the bakery, so Charles decided that they would eat out for dinner.

Charles drove Leda, Christa and Axel to their mom's bakery. As soon as she found out that they were coming, she started to tidy up and close the store.

"So, where did you all decide to have dinner?"

This time, Leda's choice was acceptable to all, so they went to their favorite pizza parlor. Axel thought... *Pizza again... I just had that for lunch. That's okay though, at least I'm home.* Leda talked about her preparations for college. She seemed excited, yet it was obvious she was feeling some anxiety about leaving home. Amazingly, Christa wanted to just relax for the rest of the summer. Axel did not realize until now how much he missed them. All in all, this was a restful, fun evening being with his family.

The chime from Axel's alarm clock woke him up at exactly eight a.m. With a smile on his face, he got dressed and gathered the things he needed for swimming. He stuffed his newly bought swim trunks, a towel, soap, and a travel sized shampoo bottle into his backpack. Satisfied with his preparation, he rushed out to the car, where his mom was waiting to drive him to Rena's house.

It was exactly nine when they arrived. Axel was about to knock on Rena's front door when he heard her say, "I'm leaving for the pool, mom," so he just waited outside. She opened the door and stepped out of the house.

"Hi, Axel. You look so… prepared?" she said with a teasing smile.

"Are you kidding? I can't wait!"

Sarah drove them to the swimming pool. Before she left, she asked them, "What time do you want me to pick you up?"

Axel replied, "How about eleven? Would that be enough time for today, Rena?"

She nodded. "Sure."

"Very well. I'll do some grocery shopping then come back for you."

Axel and Rena headed separately to the men's and women's changing areas. They put on their swimsuits and stowed their clothes in the lockers. Rena decided to start Axel in the shallow part of the pool. It was about four feet deep.

First, he did breathing exercises, until he got used to being underwater. Next, he tried floating, and then floating and paddling his legs at the same time. Surprisingly, he did not realize the strength of his legs, thanks to the rigorous training Master Soli gave him. When he paddled his legs, he was splashing so much water that the other swimmers in the pool moved away from him. Rena was laughing so hard that she patted his shoulders to make him stop.

Axel was having a great time. He realized two hours went by so fast only when Sarah was back to pick them up. On the way home, Rena said, "My cousin, Gi, has a pool in their house. It's not as big as the recreation center's pool, but their house is closer, and we can just walk there. This way, I can teach you how to swim any time."

"That'd be awesome."

Axel was very glad to learn how to swim. In just a few days, he was able to float across the width of the pool and then across the length of it. Although it was a small pool, Axel still felt good with his improvements each day.

After two weeks of swimming lessons, Axel felt a slight throb in his hand. Thankfully, it had not started to light up. He didn't want to take any chances, especially not with Rena around.

"Hey, I kinda have a headache. Do you mind if we cut this short?"

"Sure, but are you going to be okay to walk home?"

"Yeah. I'll just take some meds when I get home."

Axel got dressed as fast as he could. Rena decided to stay and have some girl time with her cousin while Axel hurriedly walked home. The pain got worse and worse over the course of dinner, but there was still no glow emanating from his palm. After eating, he gathered some snacks, his ring and sash, his journal and pen and packed them all in his backpack.

He took a bath, which was not usually part of his night routine, and then waited until dark to make his exit; but instead of leaving, he fell asleep. He woke up the next morning and realized that his hand had stopped throbbing. While a tiny part of him wondered why, he wasn't curious enough to pursue the matter. With a sigh of relief, he decided to stay home until the throbbing called for his departure again.

— CHAPTER 43 —

What Happened to Libra's Gem?

After several days of swimming and relaxing, Axel knew that the day would come when he had to go back to the other world. Besides swimming, he continued to practice running. He did not have the speed on Earth that he did in Zycodia, but at least this would strengthen his legs.

Christa's birthday was on the twenty-fifth of July, in two days. His mom and Leda were preparing a big party for her. His contribution to the party was to mow the lawn in the front and back yards. He was joyfully listening to music and mowing the law when he felt his hand start throbbing.

He frowned. This was the day he was dreading, the day when he had to go back to Zycodia and leave the comfort of his home, oh, especially his bed. That night, he begrudgingly checked his backpack to make sure he had everything he needed and, most important of all, the sash and the ring. Again, he checked if everyone was asleep. With a big sigh, he placed his hand on the tapestry and was instantly whirled away.

Exiting the tunnel, he fell flat on his face, and as he raised his head, he saw a familiar setting. He was in front of the queen's chamber, where she and Ujin were already waiting for him.

"Welcome back, Axel," Queen Elyjanah said, as she opened the door to her chambers. "How are you?"

"Except for this painful landing, I'm okay."

"Do not worry. Sooner or later, you will figure out how to make these travels less painful. For now, let's focus on the task at hand. Your mission, Axel, is to retrieve the stolen celestial gem of the Libras."

"How do I do that?"

"Ujin will take you back to Master Soli. He will provide you with all the explanations you require to succeed." She started to walk away but turned back for a moment. "Don't forget to take the belt before you go."

Axel nodded and walked over to the celestial gem room. With the belt wrapped around his waist, he ran his hand over the symbols, as he stepped out to join the queen and Ujin.

"Well, Axel, are you ready?" the queen asked.

"Not really."

Queen Elyjanah tapped his shoulder. "Best of luck, Axel. Remember, believe in yourself because I do, we all do."

Ujin then took Axel to the fifth level, through the Libra chamber, and out to ride his jet. They travelled back to Master Soli's place. It was a swift ride, and the master was already waiting for them in front of the temple. Axel stopped to look around. Flashes of his training flooded in his mind, and he shivered at the thought of each task becoming more and more difficult with every stage, wondering how he survived them all.

"Come in," said Master Soli.

Ujin and Axel climbed the stairs then walked through the hallway and into the dining area. They were given drinks while they discussed the problem.

"We had a student named Nogami from the Taurus tribe. He was very gifted and had great potential. He stayed with us for a year and a half until, one day, almost a month ago, he disappeared and never came back. We asked his parents why his training was discontinued. They just said that he was ill. Our celestial gem was set on a small altar in the prayer room. We never imagined that anyone would steal it, and it coincidentally disappeared at the same time Nogami did. I refused to believe that he stole the gem, but some of the students hesitatingly admitted that they saw him take it and hide it in his bag." Master Soli shook his head. "I think what we have to do is to go to his home and ask him why he stole the treasure and where he put it."

"Do you think he will give us an honest answer?" Ujin asked.

"He will when I'm done with him. Let's get going," Master Soli said, as he led them out of the temple. The monk's vehicle was a van big enough for ten people. Master Soli insisted that Ujin and Axel ride with him and his assistant. The van was old and clunky. Worst of all, it traveled at a snail's pace, but thanks to their trusty, expert driver, the engine powered up with its first crank. Everyone rode in silence, hearing only the banging of the engine parts.

After several miles, Axel broke the silence. "Can we go any slower?" he asked with a crack of laughter he was not able to control.

Master Soli glared at him and snorted. "How about getting out of the van and just walking?"

Axel apologized and tried hard to hide his laughter. It felt like they were riding forever, and Axel eventually fell asleep. Awakened by a sudden stop, Axel hit his head on the front seat. They arrived in the land of the Taurus, and the driver cruised slowly through the streets until they finally reached Nogami's house.

"We're here!" the driver exclaimed.

Master Soli, Ujin, and Axel got out of the bus and walked toward the house. Master Soli knocked on the door.

A lady opened it and gave a big but shy smile. "Hi, Master Soli. How nice of you to come visit us. Please come in."

She led them to the guest area. "Have a seat. Can I offer you something to eat or drink?

"No, thank you, Nita. This is Ujin, the Queen's military advisor, and this is Axel, his trainee."

Nita bowed and said, "I'm honored to meet you. What can I do for you?"

"We are here to talk to Nogami. He has been out of school for some time now, and we have some important questions to ask him."

"Would you excuse me? I'll go find Nogami." She left the room, and they heard her call Nogami. After a few minutes, Nita returned with her husband and son.

Nogami bowed to Master Soli. "Hello, Master."

"Hello, Nogami. You haven't been to school for some time now. Why have you not come back?"

"I started to not feel well, and I still do not feel good now."

"I know you are a good kid, Nogami, and I know you want to do the right thing." Master Soli paused and stared at Nogami without blinking. "I want you to tell me the truth. Did you take our celestial gem from the glass pedestal?" Master Soli level a piercing stare at Nogami.

Nogami started to cry. "I'm sorry, Master Soli. Yes, I took the celestial gem. But I had no choice! I was forced to do it!"

"By whom? What did they want with it?"

Nogami shook his head. He clearly didn't want to talk.

"Come now, Nogami, if you tell us the truth, we may be able to help you. This is Ujin, our military advisor. He has ways to help you out, isn't that right, Ujin?" he said, looking at Ujin for backup.

"Of course," Ujin said.

Nogami took a deep breath. "Digan, the notorious gangster who escaped from prison, knew I was training with you. He came to me and threatened to harm my parents if I did not get the gem. He also said that if I told anyone, I would have the same fate as my parents. As huge as he was, other folks said it took a dozen police officers to capture him. I was scared for my parents and myself, so I took the gem and gave it to him."

Master Soli sighed and gave Nogami a hug to calm him down. "Well, that shines a different light on the matter. Do you know where Digan took the celestial gem?"

"I'm not sure, but I think he has recruited some followers. They live in a compound in some mountain cave outside Taurus land. I'm sorry, Master Soli. Please forgive me."

"I'll forgive you as long as you promise to come back to us."

Nogami looked at his mom and dad then back at Master Soli. "Of course, Master Soli. Thank you so much for understanding." Nogami stopped crying and smiled with relief. He hadn't felt peace since he left the temple. Nogami timidly said, "I'd like to help you get your treasure back, but is there any way you can protect my parents? I'm afraid Digan will hurt them."

"I tell you what, you all come to the temple and stay with us while we try to retrieve our treasure and bring Digan to justice."

Nogami's dad shook his head. "I work every day. What's going to happen to my job when I do not report in?"

It was Ujin who responded to his question. "I will make sure your job will be there when this whole ordeal is over."

"We have to go now," Master Soli said. "Gather the things you would need for several days and ride with us back to the temple. I will instruct the monks to prepare the guest house for you. We live humble lives. You will be expected to help in our daily activities."

Nita said, "Of course, Master Soli, we will. Thank you very much."

Ujin cleared his throat. "Axel and I have to return to the castle. Nogami, we need you to come with us to see the queen."

Nogami was surprised. Never had he imagined he would have the chance to meet the queen. He answered excitedly, "Yes sir."

With the arrangements accepted by all, Ujin and Axel stood up and headed out. Nogami said goodbye to his mom and dad.

Ujin's jet appeared wherever he went, and it was there when they stepped out of the house. Axel was intrigued, but Nogami was taken aback by the manifestation of their transport. They rode the grand-looking jet, which, to Axel's amazement, seemed bigger than before.

"Ujin, is this your Swifty? It's different."

Ujin smiled. "You should know better by now. Here, everything may not be what it seems. Yes, this is Swifty and whether you see it or not, it follows me wherever I go. And in answer to your questioning look, it gets bigger with added seats if there are other passengers and becomes a one-seater when I'm by myself."

"That's... that's amazing. Can I have one?"

"Dream on." Ujin smiled. "You don't even know how to drive."

On the way to the castle, Axel's mind was flooded with all sorts of questions. *Would the queen have answers about what to do?* But the more important questions in his mind were: *what must he do to retrieve the celestial gem? Will he have to do it alone?* He shrugged uneasily at the thought of getting into a fight with Digan. If he was bigger than Chief Tiroh, or worse, the ogre, Axel surmised he would be dangerously in trouble.

CHAPTER 44

Nogami Meets the Queen

Nogami was excited but scared to meet Queen Elyjanah. Axel's thoughts were still focused on the looming possibility of a deadly fight with the huge Digan. True, he had defeated the ogre, but this was real life. However, knowing that Ujin, Chief Tiroh, and Master Soli were the leaders of this mission, Axel felt assured that one of them would battle Digan, especially Chief Tiroh.

Ujin took them to the lobby in front of the queen's chamber. Nogami and Axel sat on the couch to wait for her. They both stood up and were about to bow when they saw who came out of the chamber. It was Isyna. She was wearing a casual shirt and pants instead of the typical princess attire.

"Hi, hi, hi, good to see you again, Axel. I heard what you did to the ogre. I must say, you are starting to make me a believer." She turned to Nogami. "And who are you?"

"I'm Nogami."

"Mother will be out soon. See you around, Axel."

Nogami and Axel stared as she walked away.

"Wow, she's cute," Nogami exclaimed.

"Forget it, man. She's the princess," Axel said.

"Yep, out of our league, right?"

Axel nodded.

Soon after Isyna left, the queen came out, this time not in casual garb, but in her royal gown. "Nogami, I presume."

"Yes, your highness," he answered, bowing.

"How are your parents?"

"They are safe. They will be staying at Master Soli's place until this is over."

Turning to Axel, the queen asked, "Are you ready for the mission?"

Axel looked down, remembering his embarrassing failure with Amora's rescue. "Not really."

Ujin relayed everything that happened to Nogami, how the celestial gem was stolen, and who was responsible for everything. "We know it is in Digan's possession, but we have no clue where he has hidden it."

"Do you know where he is hiding?" the queen asked Nogami.

"No, I don't. His gang members took me to their hideout to deliver the gem, but I was so scared. All I can remember is that we went somewhere uphill."

Queen Elyjanah stood up and beckoned to Nogami. "Come closer and extend your hands, Nogami."

He obeyed.

"Now close your eyes."

Again, he obeyed.

She placed her hand on top of Nogami's palm. She closed her eyes and focused. Pictures started flashing through her mind. At first, they were random images, and she then realized that there was no clarity of the vision because Nogami seemed to be so nervous.

The queen opened her eyes and whispered, "Nogami, just relax. Don't be afraid, nothing will happen to you here. Take a deep breath and focus on the gem and Digan, okay?"

Nogami nodded and started thinking of all his encounters with Digan.

The most important image that the queen saw was the route to Digan's cave, and the moment Nogami handed the crystal gem to Digan. She also saw how scary and fierce-looking Digan was and the threat he posed to Nogami.

"You can open your eyes now, Nogami." She turned to Ujin, "Well, now I know where it is. Come with me."

In her chamber, there was a room that may be deemed an office. The queen turned on what looked like a computer and projected a huge map of Zycodia into the air. She traced the route she saw in Nogami's mind. It ended in a mountain outside the land of Taurus. The queen pointed to a specific location.

"This is where Digan is hiding. Bring Axel with you and go to Chief Tiroh. Tell him about the mission. Ask him for support so that he can arrest his escaped prisoner."

"Nogami wants to help with the mission as his way to make amends for what he has done. Should we bring him along?" asked Ujin.

"Has he had some training?"

"I believe he has had training with Master Soli for a year."

"Very well. Bring him along, but make sure he does not face grave danger alone."

To Nogami, she said, "Are you certain you want to join the mission?"

Nogami nodded.

"Very well, you have my permission. Be careful and always obey Ujin."

Nogami and Ujin headed out, but the queen stopped Axel. "Before you go, I have something to show you. She opened a secret compartment in the wall and pulled out what looked like a scroll.

She opened it and showed it to Axel. This time, Axel could read the words.

"Your Majesty, with the previous scrolls, I could not read the words. As soon as Elder Boscoe and Taurus leader Tiroh waved their hands, the scribbles changed to words I could read. Why is this scroll already in my language?"

"That's because this scroll has been in my possession, and I knew you would need it, so I already changed it to words you can understand.

Axel stared at the scroll and read the words.

The Chosen's hand
upon a cache to shine,
a gem to reveal
the secrets of time.

"Remember these words. You will need them when you retrieve the Libra's gem. Go now, and do your best. You have gotten the best training, so trust yourself. I know you will prevail."

He wrote the words in his journal then bowed and rushed to catch up with Ujin and Nogami.

— Chapter 45 —

The Road to Mount Paluja

It was past noon when Ujin, Axel, and Nogami reached the Taurus central district where the police station was located. It was a massive, circular building with four huge, metal doors located equal distances apart—each door representing a compass point—with glass windows that extended from door to door, fortified with bars for protection.

Ujin parked his jet in the guest space and motioned for Axel and Nogami to follow him. As they climbed the front steps, Axel noticed something that looked like a camera connected to the window. It rotated, as they got closer, like a pair of eyes watching them.

Upon reaching the top step, the huge door opened automatically, and they rushed to Chief Tiroh's office. The officers they encountered bowed to Ujin as he walked by. Some of them probably didn't know who he was, but his distinguished outfit commanded great respect.

Before they reached the office, Chief Tiroh opened the door to welcome his guests. "Ah, Ujin, welcome. What brings you here? Oh, and Axel, it's good to see you again. Come in." Looking at Nogami, he asked, "Who is this?

"This is Nogami from the Taurus tribe." They sat on the huge chairs facing the chief. Ujin began by revealing the loss of the treasure and the mission that they needed to embark on.

The chief stood up, huffing and puffing. "By the way, did you know that my butler Thom or Noby, whatever his name, was really a spy for the Cheetah Commander Dulli. He was ordered to kidnap Amora in exchange for our gem. Both Dulli and Noby were subjects of Sevion. Because he failed to get our gem, the next day my men saw him dead in his cell."

"As for that notorious, disgraceful gangster, I'll be dammed if I won't join your assault. I want him back in my jail. Do you have any idea where to find him?"

"Yes, the queen retrieved all the information from Nogami. He is hiding in one of the caves of Mount Paluja."

"Ah, makes sense. Those caves are hidden by a dense forest." He huffed again. "No matter. He can't hide from us. Wherever he is, we'll find him."

He walked to his desk and pressed the button on his communication device. "Bokker, gather up your men. We have an urgent mission. Just leave a few officers in the station."

From the intercom, an excited "yes, sir" crackled loudly. One could even imagine that Bokker was rigidly saluting with his answer.

The angry chief started collecting weapons from his safe. "Time to go!"

Before they could leave the room, six individuals wearing monk robes rushed towards them. Leading the group was Master Soli.

Ujin seemed surprised. "Why are you here?"

"We have come to join your mission. While it is Chief Tiroh's goal to capture Digan, ours is to retrieve our treasure."

"How did you know about it?"

"I got a message from Queen Elyjanah."

"But you have no weapons, so how can you fight?" Chief Tiroh interjected.

Master Soli grinned. "Oh, that's right. You have never seen us in action, have you?

"No, I have not."

"You will be surprised at what we can do," Master Soli replied with a smile.

Tiroh shrugged in response and said, "Okay, the more the merrier."

Ujin smiled. He knew that Master Soli and the monks were skilled in combat. "Chief Tiroh, now that Master Soli's group is here to join our mission, let's go over my plan of attack."

Ujin walked toward the huge desk and produced a small, flattened, pyramidal gadget from his coat. He pressed a button on one of the sides, and an image projected upward. "This is a map of Mount Paluja and all the surrounding areas. If I turn this remote around, you can see the entire area from the north, south, east or west."

His audience came closer, going around the table to get a view from all sides.

With his hand pointing at the spots, he continued, "This road is Pacq Road. It is connected to the main highway, Route Q, from Taurus's downtown about fifteen miles away, and, as you can see, it heads onto the path east of the mountain toward the cave, which is this dark area, right here. There is a clearing in front of the entrance." Ujin turned to face Tiroh. "Chief Tiroh, since the main highway goes through the south and intersects with the main path that goes through the east. Go south and then most of your men can charge from the east, but assign a few of them to climb up the side of the cave and jump to join the attack."

Chief Tiroh nodded. "Okay, makes sense. That path is wide enough for us. And while we are in battle with his men, those coming down from that up there," he pointed to the spot, "will box them in."

Ujin nodded. "Now, the section from the south to the west side of Mount Paluja is dense and full of trees. There is no pathway toward the cave through this side of the mountain, but with your legendary power and skills, Master Soli, you and your men can easily manage going up. While Chief Tiroh charges from the opposite side, an attack by your group would surely surprise Digan."

"Well, it would take but a few minutes for us to get there," he estimated.

"Very good. Master Soli, once your group touches down in this section, wait until Chief Tiroh's group reaches the cave. I will follow next and enter through this narrow pathway to the cave with Axel and Nogami. This is a straight path just below the cave. We will wait until Master Soli gets into position. To coordinate the timing, here are communicators for each of you. They are all set to the right frequency. When you get to the designated points, press this button and utter the code signal *'dinner is ready.'*"

He handed one to Master Soli and another one to the chief. "Master Soli, once you get to that point, give us the signal. That will be the time for you and your men, chief, to get into position, then communicate the signal."

"Chief, when you hear that Master Soli say the code signal, begin your attack. When you are ready to charge, what code signal do you want to use?"

Chief Tiroh said, "How about *'time to eat?'*"

Everyone laughed.

Chief Tiroh smiled. "Why not? It'll be time to eat Digan."

"Fine. Master Soli, when the battle starts, wait until Digan's men are engaged before your assault. Axel, Nogami, and I are to follow shortly. Do you have any questions?"

Chief Tiroh answered quickly, "No, let's go. No time to waste. I want Digan back in my jail or dead, whichever comes first." He armed himself with as many weapons as he could carry. Like a posse, they all marched out with the firm determination to win this battle.

When they exited the front door, they saw around three dozen police officers seated on their bikes, powered up, and ready to go. With helmets on their heads and weapons hanging all over their bodies, they were an awesome sight.

Ujin asked the chief, "Is everyone here?"

He nodded with pride at seeing his brave men determined and prepared for battle.

Surprisingly, Axel saw Isyna standing by a bike, wearing an armorlike outfit with a sword tucked in her belt. Rushing down the steps, he asked, "Isyna, why are you here? Are you joining this mission?" As much as he did not like Isyna, he was concerned that the queen might not approve of what she was doing.

"Someone needs to babysit you and maybe even save you if needed," she said sarcastically.

"Huh, maybe I'll be the one saving you," he retorted then ran back to Nogami and Ujin.

Ujin moved up to address troops. "Listen, everyone. I thank you all for your readiness. Our destination is Mount Paluja, east of Taurus land, and our goal is the recapture of Digan. I'm sure you all know him. Master Soli and his fellow monks will join us. I will be coordinating the mission with Chief Tiroh and Master Soli. Nogami and Axel will stay with me. Is that understood?"

A resounding chorus yelled, "yes, sir!"

"Now, let's roll."

Master Soli's group rushed to their bus. Axel wondered how their super slow vehicle would make it in time ahead of everyone else. As the driver cranked up the engine, it bolted faster than its usual speed.

Next to exit was Chief Tiroh, who rode in his police jeep with his deputy and was followed by his men. From left and right, they drove in rows of four toward the road. It was an army on the march, a sight Axel only saw in movies. The reality of being in a real battle was causing him so much anxiety. He was unsure of what else he was feeling, but he knew that turning away was not an option.

Ujin turned his attention to Isyna. "Are you sure you want to join our mission?"

She nodded.

Ujin said, "I prefer you ride with us instead of going on your own."

So Isyna joined Axel and Nogami in Ujin's jet. Before he powered the engine, he made a call to someone Axel didn't know. Nogami, who had the same questioning look on his face, nudged Axel. Axel knew it was not his place to be so inquisitive at this time, so he shrugged, indicating he had no clue.

With the speed of the Ujin's jet, the bikes, and the jeep, they reached their destination in less than an hour and parked half a mile from Mount Paluja. The clanking sounds of Master Soli's van announced their arrival a few minutes later. Ujin signaled for them to move to the west side of the cave.

Upon reaching a hidden spot, the driver parked the van and turned off the engine. The sounds gradually ebbed to a stop. With Master Soli on the lead, the monks transformed into owls and flew to the designated spot that was just behind the cave. This transformation was such a sight to behold. As they landed, one by one, they reverted to their human forms. Master Soli clicked the communicator and quietly said, *"Dinner is ready."*

Hearing their code, Chief Tiroh signaled his men to move toward the bottom of the mountain. They immediately dismounted from their vehicles. The pumped-up chief held up his communicator and said, *"Dinner is ready."* Too impatient to wait for Ujin's signal, he announced excitedly, *"Time to Eat."* With that shout, he raised his hand to the troops, and they began charging toward the cave.

From where Ujin, Isyna, Axel, and Nogami were positioned, they saw the monks and police offices shift their forms. It was remarkable to see them each magically transform into raging bulls. The roaring thunder of their hoofs shook the mountain like an earthquake. They raced faster and faster, and in no time, they had almost reached the clearing.

CHAPTER 46

The Rebels

The entrance to the cave was wide but inconspicuous to anyone passing though Route Q from Taurus territory. Although there was a wide clearing in front of it, huge trees below it covered the view. Inside, the walls were plain, the floor was paved, and because the ventilation was not good, the atmosphere was stuffy. Cots were lined up in common areas and there were tables and benches where they dined.

The escaped prisoner, Digan, was the commander of a group named The New Rebels. He was as huge as Chief Tiroh. His dark, piercing, beady eyes were settled just above a large, round nose, and wide mouth. He was vain about his shoulder-length hair and had his assistant comb it every day.

The New Rebels were composed of twenty male and four female members. Most of them came from Taurus land, and a few came from other tribes. He had a bed in his small but private chamber where he was relaxing. Some members were taking naps and others were eating. A few of them were playing card games. Discipline was not strictly enforced, but if at any time, any one of them defied Digan's orders, there was no mercy given.

From above the cave, Errol, Digan's trusty guard, was keeping an eye out for any danger. He had been lazily scanning the horizon for the past hour, when a sudden movement in the east grabbed his attention. Errol raised his small spyglass and focused on the movement. He nearly dropped the spyglass in alarm and scrambled down his perch, calling for Digan.

"What's the matter?" Digan came out of his room.

Errol was out of breath. "Out there—there… there are…" He gasped, handed Digan his spyglass, and pointed.

"What?" Digan was getting irritated by Errol's inability to talk. Digan grabbed the instrument and went out of the cave. Peering through it, he saw the military vehicles parked down the mountain and the charging bulls coming from the east.

"Darn it!" He snorted. "Everyone, get ready. We are being raided."

Digan's gang was unprepared. Those eating at the dining tables left their food and jumped out of their seats. Hokat, Digan's second in command, ran to the sleeping room to wake up those who were napping. Once the realization of imminent danger hit their minds, they jumped up and scampered around to grab their weapons and shields. They were so disorganized they bumped into each other.

Hokat tried his best to direct the traffic flow. Those who were not already armed had to get their weapons from a secured area. Once they were ready, they were directed to run along one side of the cave to face their attackers.

Digan armed himself with a sword and two guns in a double holster around his chest. He rushed out in front of everyone shouting, "Are you all strong to fight?"

"Yeah!" they all shouted in unison and raised their fists.

Errol followed closely behind his boss carrying knives. The rest of the gang trailed, some excited, some scared, but all ready to go.

Unbeknownst to anyone, the psychic eye of Sevion watched everything that was going on. With his magical power, he blew the wind to create a cloud of dust in the entrance of the cave.

— CHAPTER 47 —

The Battle Begins

The transformed Taurus troops huffed and puffed, racing up the hill faster and faster. As they approached the clearing in front of the cave, Digan's men, led by Errol, came rushing out to face them.

Some of them morphed into bulls, but those who did not positioned themselves behind trees and big rocks with their weapons aimed at the raiders.

Digan fired the first shot, but no one was hit. He commanded, "Shoot, shoot!"

His men aimed and fired.

With the speed of Chief Tiroh's troops, none of the shots hit them, and, in a short time, they came face to face with their enemies. Horns locked, they struggled and tumbled.

The strong fighters got up and pounced on their opponents. The weaker ones got crushed. Dust was everywhere as, one by one, Digan's fighters were sent rolling down the mountain. The officers were down to the last one when a second batch of Digan's men came rushing out of the cave.

As this next batch came charging out, four of Chief Tiroh's officers who had climbed through the north side to surprise the enemies transformed, as they pounced down in pairs. Upon contact, they clamped their horns to the transformed bulls' hind legs and tossed them upward.

The troops that were charging in immediately got out of the way when bodies started somersaulting down the mountain. Some of Digan's remaining men tried to escape through a secret exit door. Unfortunately for them, Chief Tiroh discovered the exit and had already posted a few men on the other side of the mountain.

Digan watched in horror and anger as his men were defeated.

— CHAPTER 48 —

The Monks' Legendary Skills

Ujin, who was climbing the narrow path with Axel and Nogami, heard Master Soli in the communicator, "Ujin, it's our time to eat!"

As fast as the wind, the monks came out of hiding, transformed into owls, and attacked those positioned behind the trees and rocks. Digan's troops toppled over, giving the monks a chance to revert to human form. With their martial arts skills, the monks effortlessly knocked down the enemies.

Master Soli thought the fight was over, but three bulls rushed out of the cave, stopping when they saw the monks. They shifted to human form and had big smiles on their faces. Clearly, they thought defeating these small monks would be so easy that there was no need to transform.

With their foot-long rods, the brave monks faced their opponents. Three monks jabbed their enemies' stomachs while the others swept their legs, knocking them to the ground.

This downfall made the gang members irate, and they transformed themselves into raging bulls and started to charge at them. Master Soli signaled the monks to change into owls, and they swiftly flew up the trees, disappearing. The bulls could not stop their momentum. Their impact with the trees was so strong that they toppled over and collapsed.

Digan saw this blunder and ordered his remaining members to fight the monks. Surprisingly, those sent out had some sparring skills that made the confrontation last longer than Master Soli expected.

The monks shifted back and forth from human to owl to human. In human form, they punched and then morphed into owls as they kicked the enemy's heads. Not knowing if it was the monk or the owl that was attacking them, Digan's men collided with each other and were knocked down by the agile monks.

— CHAPTER 49 —

The Battle Ends

Seeing his men get beaten one by one, the angry Digan huffed and puffed in front of his cave. He saw Ujin climbing up the narrow pathway and ordered Hokat to confront the incoming assault with a sword. Hokat obeyed and jumped down to attack Ujin, who countered with a special laser sword. Their weapons clashed—a hit, a block, another hit and another block. The fight went on.

Nogami and Axel climbed up, trying to hit every enemy along the way with the foot-long rods they got from Master Soli. This was when a mysterious dust cloud circled the mountain, making it hard to see and distinguish friend from foe.

Digan's gang was no match for the brute force of Chief Tiroh's troops and the fighting skills of Master Soli's group. They dropped down one after another, except for Digan and his right-hand man, Hokat, who was fighting Ujin.

As strong as he was, Digan was hard to beat. Chief Tiroh tried to subdue him but failed. Digan charged forward zigzagging down the mountain. He was getting away. Axel was almost knocked down, but he regained his balance. Seeing everyone engaged in fights, including Ujin, Isyna, and Nogami, Axel decided to pursue Digan.

His adrenaline pumping, Axel jumped up and chased after Digan, employing his Cancer speed and Taurus strength. Digan was about to escape when Axel caught up to him. He jumped on Digan's back, dragging them both to the ground. After a short while, Digan and Axel both got up. To his shock, Digan shifted to a bull. He huffed and puffed, faced Axel, and kicked forward to charge. As soon as he got close to Axel, with a swift evasive move to the left, Axel swung the rod upward with all his strength and hit

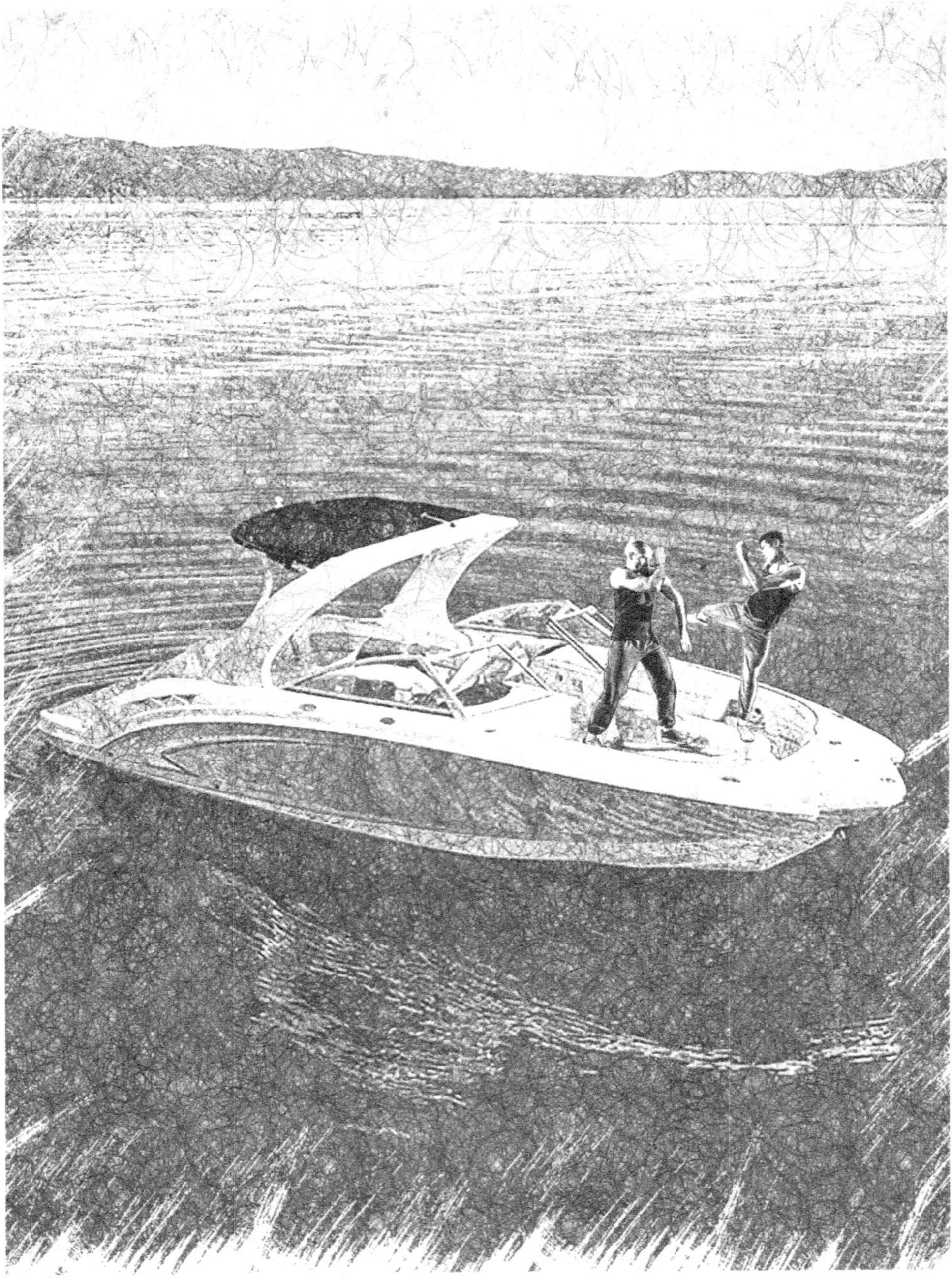

Digan's neck, making him fall backwards. That maneuver hurt his arm, and he fell to the ground.

Digan recovered and ran towards the lake, where he'd hidden a motorboat to aid in his escape. He untied the boat, powered the engine, and sailed as fast as it could toward the island across the water.

By the time Axel recovered, Digan was already in the middle of the lake. Looking around for help, Axel realized the site of the battle was far away, and no one else was close enough to pursue the enemy. Axel mustered his strength and ran towards the lake. A momentary doubt stuck his mind, and his resolve was shaken, when suddenly, he seemed to hear the voice of the Queen saying, "Axel, believe in yourself. I believe in you." He looked around to see if the queen was there with him and saw no one. "You may not see me, but I am there with you."

Hearing these words, Axel took a deep breath and, with his power of speed combined with the swimming lessons from Rena, he rapidly swam towards Digan's boat. Upon reaching it, he hauled himself over the edge, causing the boat to rock. Digan turned around and stepped closer to punch him. Master Soli's torturous training with the cones helped Axel maintain his balance on the rocking boat, while his training with the robots helped him skillfully block every punch Digan threw at him.

As the boat continued to rock, the big and heavy Digan, unable to balance himself, fell overboard into the lake. Axel grabbed an oar attached to the side of the boat and knocked out Digan. Worried that Digan's weight would make him sink, Axel used his remaining strength to pull Digan back into the boat. He restrained his arms for good measure.

Because he did not know how to operate the motorboat, and didn't have enough strength left to paddle to shore, he decided to stay put until someone could rescue them.

After several minutes, Axel saw a jet coming towards them. It was Ujin in his Swifty. A hatch opened from the jet's tail, and a hook clamped to the boat. The jet slowly towed the boat back to the shore.

Chief Tiroh and his men were ready to receive the arrivals. When Digan came to, he was handcuffed and dragged to an armored vehicle.

Axel grabbed a rod a police officer was holding and rushed to the vehicle holding Digan. He punched Digan and pressed the rod into Digan's neck. "Where's Master Soli's treasure?" Digan kept his silence, so Axel continued punching him until he relented. Defeated, Digan revealed the location of the gem.

As soon as Axel stepped out and closed the vehicle's door, an image appeared in front of Digan, who bowed and fearfully exclaimed, "Lord Sevion, I am so sorry I lost."

Sevion was irate. He used his psychic power to contort Digan's body and repeatedly ram it into the walls of the vehicle until he collapsed. Chief Tiroh heard the commotion and rushed to open the door. He was taken aback by the dissipating image of Sevion and Digan's lifeless body. Not wanting others to see what happened, he rapidly closed the door.

Everyone cheered their victory. All the gang members were rounded up and placed in a Taurus bus that had just arrived.

"Good job, Axel," Ujin said. "Did he tell you where he hid the gem?"

"Yes, this way," he said and painstakingly climbed up the mountain with Ujin, Chief Tiroh, and Master Soli following behind him. Even Isyna rushed to join the team. They went inside the cave, and Axel told them where to look. The cave was a bit dark. Ujin handed a small pointer to Axel. Axel used it to light up the walls.

Axel did a thorough search, running his hand along the walls. "Ujin, there's an inner section over here. Looks like the wall is covered with bricks."

He moved the beam across the wall, searching for the brick that could be the gem's hiding place. He began tapping on each one when, suddenly, one brick that was larger than all the rest caught his eye. Following his instincts, he pushed it inward. It did not budge. He tried it again and again, but still, it did not open. He noticed that the smaller ones on the left and right sides were loose. He pushed them both inward—surprise—the large one in the middle popped halfway out.

Axel pulled the brick out and laid it on the ground. "Ujin, Master Soli, it's here!" He extracted the small, black box that was inside.

Chief Tiroh said anxiously, "Does anyone have the key to open this box?"

"No, only Axel can," Ujin said.

Tiroh scoffed. "What are you waiting for? Come on, open it."

Ujin signaled to Axel. "Go ahead. Open it. I assume Queen Elyjanah revealed to you what to do with this box."

Axel remembered the words on the scroll: *the chosen hand, upon a cache to shine; a gem to reveal the secrets of time.* He took a deep breath. His nervousness was obvious, as he laid his shaking hand on top. As the box opened, it emitted a bright light that temporarily blinded them. The celestial gem's light ebbed until the gem looked like a regular stone. Master Soli came closer to pick it up. He examined it to make sure that it was their lost treasure. Convinced of its authenticity, he showed this two-piece Libra scale to all of them.

Master Soli said, "This precious gem has the power of time and balance. Luckily, Digan could not open the box and use this gem's power. This is a joyous victory, indeed." He rejoiced in its recovery but placed it back inside the box and gave it to Axel. "Thank you, Axel, for your help in retrieving our treasure. For now, I believe you are the one who is going to need this."

Axel reluctantly accepted the box.

Ujin nodded. "Now, we must go back to the castle."

They exited the cave and went down the mountain, where everyone was eagerly waiting for their leaders. To everyone's surprise, a majestic jet arrived. The queen had traveled to Mount Paluja to greet the victorious team. She wore a simple crown and a gown with a cape over. She stepped out of her jet, aided by Ujin, and looked at everyone kneeling in her appearance. She signaled for them to rise. "Congratulations. Great job, everyone."

The queen looked at Axel. "I feared for your life when I saw you run after Digan, but you bravely faced the danger."

"Your Highness, thank you for your words when I was near the lake. They gave me the strength to do what I believed needed to be done."

"I'm glad I was able to reach out and help." She turning and gave her daughter a big hug. "I am also very proud of you."

Isyna proudly stated, "With me there, they had no chance."

That gave everyone a chuckle.

Isyna whispered to Axel, "Well, I can say I was glad you defeated Digan. Don't get me wrong, you still have other battles to face, and I'm still holding on to my opinion of you."

Axel responded with just a smile, thinking, *I'm also reserving my opinion of you.*

Seeing the queen's signal, Chief Tiroh approached her and bowed. "Your majesty, what can I do for you?"

She asked, "What happened to Digan?"

"I am sorry, your highness. Digan is dead. Of course, we arrested him, but we heard a loud commotion inside the vehicle. When I opened the door, I could not believe what I saw. A fading image of Sevion loomed over Digan's dead body."

"Thank you for that information," she replied with a concerned look then waved to Isyna to enter her jet. "Ujin, I shall wait for you at the castle."

Master Soli interjected, "Nogami, you showed great courage." To Axel, he said, "Take care of our treasure. Use it only for good."

Axel stared at the box he was holding. He was so elated that he could not find words to answer his mentor.

Ujin shook the master's hand and thanked him for helping make the mission a success. He then patted Axel on the back and said, "Let's go back to the castle."

Master Soli signaled to his group to get ready to return to their vehicle. One of the monks grabbed Nogami, told him to hold on, and transformed into an owl. The monks all flew down to the roadside in their owl forms then changed back. After Nogami shakily entered the van, they headed back to their temple.

Chief Tiroh ordered his men to start moving. He led the first pack, which was followed by the bus filled with Digan's men and guarded by the second pack of officers. Although they looked exhausted, the satisfaction and pride of winning was evident in their faces.

CHAPTER 50

A Vision Through Time

Back in her quarters, Queen Elyjanah held the Libra tribe's treasure in her hand. She asked, "Did Master Soli reveal to you the power of this gem?"

"Master Soli said this holds the power of time and balance."

"Yes, that is correct. Bonding with it will allow you to travel to any time and to wherever your heart desires. When you decide to take that step, it will be an amazing experience you will never forget. You will get the gift of balance, time, and space, but be warned, you can use this power only under the most desperate situations."

"Now, if you do not have any questions, go inside. This time place the gem on your head."

Axel hesitated. "If I make that travel, how will I come back?"

"Oh, don't worry about that. Once you've seen what you need to see, you will return to our time."

"What if I do not see that what I'm supposed to see?"

The queen tried to reassure him. "You'll see it for sure, and if the time has come, and you are not back, I will rescue you. Is that good enough?"

Axel nodded.

He went inside the sacred room. Queen Elyjanah gave him the celestial gem then left the room.

Axel placed the gem on his head. It was as if the light switch was turned on, and the glow became brighter and brighter. At the same time, it enveloped his head and crept down to enclose his entire body. At this point, he felt as if the world was spinning around. He became dizzy and fell unconscious.

Disoriented, when he opened his eyes, he realized he was no longer in the sacred room. He was lying on the grass, and it was nighttime, but where? He adjusted his eyes to the surroundings and realized he was in a familiar place. It was their village. It looked a bit different, but it was undoubtedly the same town plaza. He came closer to where everyone was gathered. It was almost midnight, and people were waiting for the fireworks.

Surprisingly, he saw his dad and mom. He also saw two girls with them and realized they were Leda and Christa as little girls. They were very young and his mom… surprise, surprise …his mom was pregnant.

He went closer and tested to see if they could see him by shaking his hand in front of their faces, no reaction. No one could see him.

Sarah started moaning and told Charles that she was having labor pains. The cramping started. Suddenly, all the lights went out. Music stopped. People were scampering around to find flashlights or candles. While the chaos was going on, the frequency of Sarah's cramping was increasing by the minute. Charles looked for Dr. Trent to let him know that he had to take Sarah to the hospital because she may have the baby soon.

Charles supported Sarah in the car while the girls rushed inside. The doctor rushed to get his medical bag and drove his station wagon behind them. Axel tried to follow but was transported to an open field. Their car had stalled. Sarah was moaning in pain. His dad tried to fix the car but because it was too dark, he gave up. Instead, he opened the trunk and got a flashlight.

Sarah's contractions became more and more frequent. She told Charles the baby was coming. He gave the flashlight to Leda to hold. He supported Sarah as he pressed the lever of the seat to go down backwards. Charles got a coat and put it under Sarah.

Dr. Trent stopped his car and ran towards her.

Charles handed a bottle of alcohol to the doctor, who used it to clean his hands. He helped Sarah get out of the car. He laid a blanket on the grass where she painstakingly laid down.

"Leda, give me the flashlight."

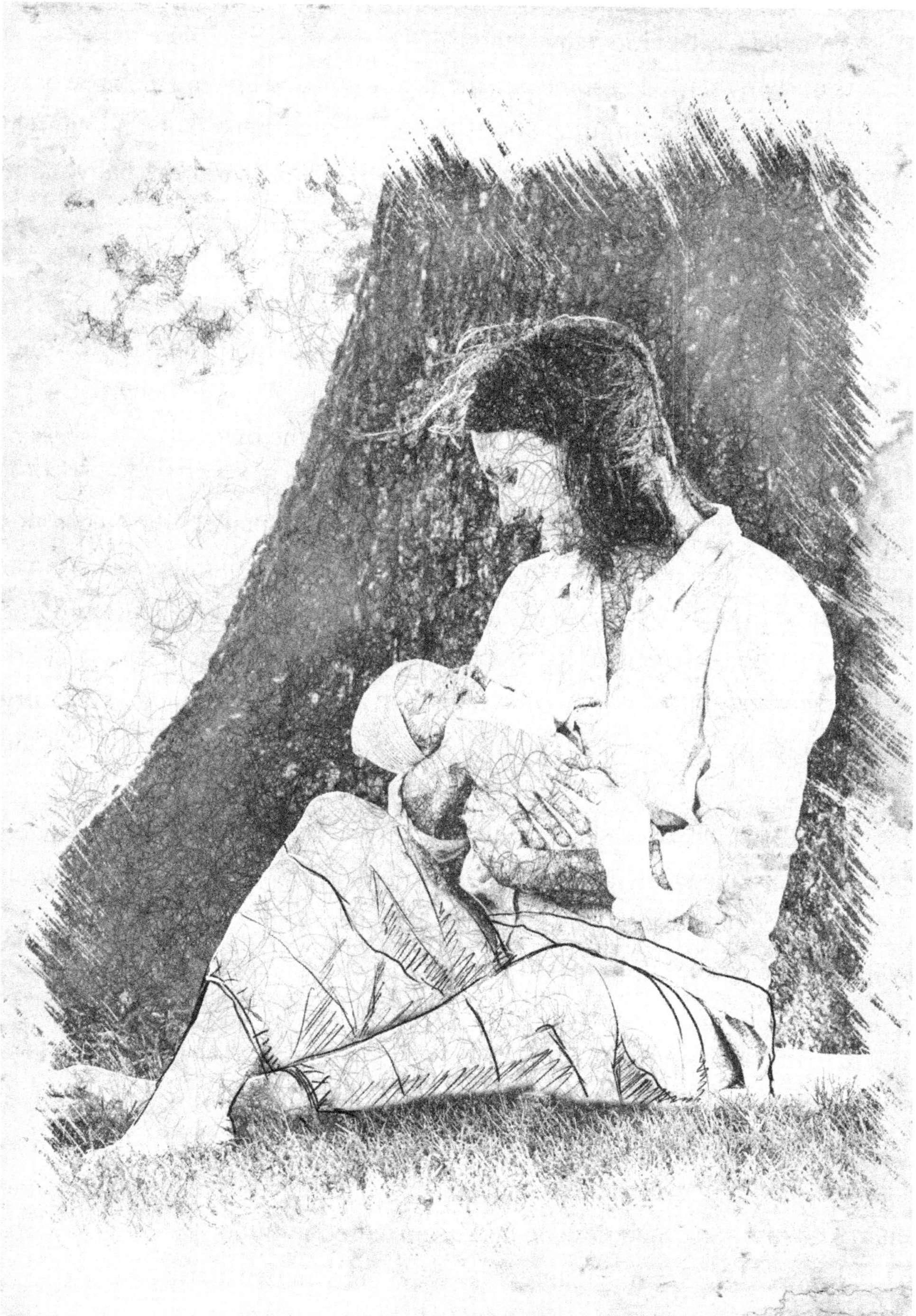

Leda was only four years old and scared, but she did as she was told.

"You and Christa move over there."

As the baby started to come out, the sky brightened up with the fireworks. Suddenly, a bright beam lit up above them. They all looked up and thought it was a comet passing by. Sarah laboriously pushed until the baby came out.

Charles smiled. "Sarah, it's a boy!"

Dr. Trent gave the baby light taps on the back, and he started crying.

Tears flowed down Sarah's cheeks, and she was too exhausted to smile back.

"Leda, give me the other blanket that's inside the bag."

She unzipped the bag and handed the blanket to her dad.

Charles wrapped the baby with the blanket and placed him in Sarah's extended arms. He kissed Sarah's forehead and gazed lovingly at his son.

Amazingly, the sky was still bright with fireworks, but amid the explosions, the sky seemed to be opening. A woman emerged from the dark hole. She was wearing a long, flowing gown and almost seemed like a fairy from old children's stories. The lady slowly descended and landed on the ground.

Axel came closer to see who the lady was. To his surprise, he realized the lady was Queen Elyjanah. Even more to his surprise, Charles and Sarah could not see her. However, Leda and Christa could.

Leda cried out, "Dad, there's a lady up there."

"Where?"

"There," Christa pointed.

"There's no one there," Charles said, looking around him.

Leda and Christa were staring at Queen Elyjanah, as she bent down to kiss the baby's forehead. She touched his right hand as if pressing some energy to him. She then flew up and disappeared into the sky.

Charles looked at his daughters. "What are you two staring at?"

Leda said, "The lady touched the baby's hand."

Christa nodded. "But she flew away."

Charles shook his head, ignored what Leda and Christa were saying, and bent down to kiss Sarah and the baby again.

Soon, the ambulance came. The paramedics brought out the stretcher and their bags to check on the baby and Sarah. One of them checked the baby's heartbeat with his stethoscope and took his temperature. The paramedic said, "Congratulations, your baby boy seems to be healthy. Do you have a name for your baby?"

"Axel. His name is Axel," Sarah whispered as she was laid on the stretcher and raised into the ambulance.

Axel was in awe of what he just saw. He had just witnessed his own birth!

As the three vehicles moved on, the scenery faded. Axel again felt like he was spinning around and when it stopped, he found himself back in the sacred room sitting on one of the steps of the pedestal.

"Do you remember what just happened? What did you see?" Queen Elyjanah asked when he stepped out of the room.

"Yes. I remember," he answered shakily. He sat down to calm his nerves. "I saw what happened when I was born. I saw you come down and kiss the baby's forehead—my forehead—and touch my hand. Then you disappeared back in the sky."

"Yes, what you witnessed was your birth. When my father died, I decided to visit Earth to see the prophesized son who would have a destiny in Zycodia. My touching your hand was the imprint marking your connection to our world."

Axel had a nagging question. "What happened when I turned one? I was told that one of the fireworks hit my right hand, and that is the reason I have this scar."

"The spark that hit your right hand was from our celestial orb transferring energy to your hand. This gem that you bonded with now gave you the power of time. In fact, with this celestial gem, you can now travel here any time you want or need to."

Axel felt the gem now imbedded on the belt as it floated back in its place.

"Just remember, though. It would be best for now that no one knows about your flights to our world."

"No one would believe me anyway. Thank you for everything. Thanks to you also, Ujin. Please give my thanks to Rolin, too. He gave me some pretty good advice."

"Until next time, Axel, be well."

Axel said goodbye and then opened the portal. He floated back through the tunnel. This time, he did not feel like he was being sucked in. Knowing the connection he had with this world, this time he felt in balance and at peace, until he popped out of the tapestry and fell on the floor.

"Ouch!" he cried.

Opening his eyes, he was utterly shocked to see someone's feet in front of him. Slowly lifting his eyes, he saw a big smirk on Christa's face.

"Aha!"

The End

Made in the USA
Las Vegas, NV
08 February 2025